MAID(S)

maid

NOUN \\'MāD\\

1. **Mother (s) addicted to Irish Dancing**

BRENNA BRIGGS

Dedication
This book is dedicated to MAIDS
and others struggling with addictions.

Disclaimer
This is a work of fiction.
You will not find yourself
in this book. If you do think you see yourself,
seek help.

There may be Gorgons to encounter, and monsters
of the deep... Louis Tracy

Acknowledgements

Thanks to the ancient Greek playwrights, Aristophanes, for his wonderful comedies, and Euripides, for his mind boggling tragedies. Their plays have greatly influenced some of the characters in this book. Greek mythological traditions of 'female' creatures, such as Gorgons and Harpies, were inspirational. Author/ Attorney T. Evan Williams' advice as to the distinctions between libel and slander defamation were invaluable. As was his editing.

The Ten MAIDS
(Mothers Addicted to Irish Dancing)

Jessica: Team Mother
Dana: Team Mother
Brandi: Mother of Sub #2
Sylvia: Mother of Sub #1
Valerie: Team Mother
Michelle: Team Mother
Stacey: Team Mother
Sarah: Team Mother
Linda: Team Mother
Melissa: Team Mother

The Others

Irish Dance Mothers who have not yet become MAIDS

The Ten DDS

Dancing Daughters

The T.C.R.G.

The Certified Irish Dance Teacher

The Letter-Writer: Unknown

This book is also dedicated to the men who have devoted themselves to their Irish dancers.

Especially, Kevin McCaughley.

Introducing Jessica

$\mathcal{B}$reathing slowly had finally centered Jessica. She was prepared now to have Siri call 911.

Jessica's migraine was debilitating, but the flashing lights and zigzag lightning bolts had finally stopped by the time she managed to kneel down on the white-tiled kitchen floor next to her twelve-year-old daughter.

Catelyn was curled up in the fetal position, a trickle of blood dribbling from the corner of her mouth, like baby slobber running down a plastic bib.

Jessica tried to keep it together. She could not start hyperventilating or risk having a panic attack. She had to be here now for her daughter. She placed her phone on the kitchen table and instructed Siri to call 911.

"Help is on their way," the 911 dispatcher said, in what seemed like a fraction of a second.

"What is your emergency?"

Jessica explained her daughter's status.

"I need you to kneel down on the floor beside your daughter..." Jessica's thoughts wandered.

Duh! What kind of mother would just stand there looking down at her daughter on the floor?

After Jessica had verified that her daughter was not conscious, the dispatcher inquired, as calmly as if she were asking for the time of day, "Can you tell if she is breathing?"

What if Catelyn were not breathing? Would she be expected to perform CPR with all that blood?

Jessica, placing her right hand below her daughter's ribcage, could feel the almost imperceptible expansion and contraction of Catelyn's diaphragm.

"Yes. She's breathing."

"Does her breathing sound normal?"

Jessica was worried about her own breathing which was becoming labored. Blood always made her angry. She begrudgingly moved closer to her daughter's nose, but not so close as to risk getting blood stains on her Eskander white cotton blouse.

"Yes. I think so."

"Good. Is there a trace of blood coming from any orifices? Her ears, mouth or nose?"

Jessica felt a bit awkward about not having revealed the blood detail to the 911 dispatcher. It made her look

2

unobservant and careless, which she certainly was not.

"Yes. I do see some blood in the right corner of her mouth."

"You need to…" Jessica detached again. The stress was getting to her. She began to lose her composure. She could feel her chest tightening up, thinking about how difficult it was to remove blood stains from white cotton. If she acted immediately, she might be able to prevent a breathing problem of her own that she often experienced in the midst of a Catelyn health crisis.

She reached for the emergency brown paper lunch bag secreted in the napkin holder on the kitchen table. It had been carefully folded, so as not to detract from the lemon-yellow paper napkins. Anticipating the next seizure episode was very important and she liked to be well-prepared.

Proceeding with extreme caution, taking great care to properly seal off her thin-lipped mouth and Roman nose, she carefully positioned the lunch bag and began to slowly inhale and exhale. What possible help could she be to her daughter in this situation if she herself passed out from oxygen deprivation?

Catelyn's falling down like this has got to stop! she thought, breathing the lunch bag's stale air in and puffing it out.

If the regional neurological doctors clinic did not soon diagnose her daughter, then she would take her to the Mayo Clinic. If the Mayo Clinic could not do the job, then she might go to Europe. Or India, where she had read blogs about herbal medicine often being tried there before resorting to synthetic drugs.

Breathing into the brown paper bag was helping her think clearly again. Her lightheadedness was receding.

She removed the paper bag and took a deep breath. She would never let her daughter down.

Jessica elevated her daughter's floppy head, after she had carefully tucked her new blouse into her beige bra, and ripped the lunch bag apart to cover her lap.

Her girl had never needed her more. Especially now that Catelyn's U-13 8-Hand Céilí Team had scheduled intense, grueling practices over the next four weeks, preparing for the World Irish Dance Championships.

Catelyn's U-13 céilí team was a tight unit—inspiring really—but it was hard not to be concerned about Catelyn's solo steps, and especially her Slip Jig. It was still a disgrace. The pathetic coach Jessica had hired to straighten out her daughter's soft shoe mess would be let go without pay by the end of this week if Catelyn's technique did not dramatically improve by then.

Dancers who had qualified to do their solo steps at the Worlds had worked very hard to get there. She was not about to let her DD slip through the cracks after all the work that both of them had put in over the last few years.

Faraway sirens alerted Jessica to untuck her cotton blouse from her bra and prepare for the medics arrival.

Using one of the lemon-yellow paper napkins, she wiped up some, but not all of the disgusting blood on the floor. If the EMTs stepped in it, they might stain the cornflower blue throw rug.

Introducing Dana

$\mathcal{D}$ana tried not to show how concerned she was that her daughter, Kaitlin, was noticeably shorter than the other girls on her U-13 8-Hand Céilí Team which had, for the first time, qualified for the World Irish Dance Championships.

Recently, it had become obvious that her child was even shorter than that #1 Sub for the U-13 Céilí Team, whose name Dana could never remember. The Sub's mother, Sylvia, was always interrupting conversations, butting in with her unwanted advice, probably because she was an attorney and expected to be paid for it.

After waiting futilely all year for signs of a growth spurt like the other DDs were exhibiting, Dana had decided to contact a pediatric endocrinologist about her concerns. If Kaitlin's blood work looked good, the next step would be rGH synthetic hormone shots.

Kaitlin had, since birth, always been at the bottom of growth developmental milestone charts. A Google search had revealed that this indicated she would never be much taller than four feet eleven inches. *Like we are seriously living in some third world country where children never get enough to eat?* She gritted her teeth in frustration.

Dana had tried over the last twelve years, to forget about the questionable World Health Organization's International Growth Standards.

These so-called 'standards' only applied to infants living in environments believed to support what the WHO research geniuses decided to be the 'optimal growth' of children in six countries, including the U.S.

Dana could not remember the other five countries because, according to Gert, her therapist, after Kaitlin had been born and up until now, she had blocked this useless information to protect her delicate emotional condition—her acute disappointment.

The World Health Organization called it longitude. *What kind of growth chart talks about a baby's 'longitude?'*

The WHO height distribution charts showed how infants and young children were supposed to grow under the best conditions. And you had to breastfeed to even be included in their statistics. WHO growth charts only reflected growth patterns among children who were mostly breastfed up until the child was at least one year old.

Like anyone would ever actually *do* that.

Therapist Gert had somehow gotten her through the black rages incited by her pediatrician every time she had taken her infant daughter in for a well-baby checkup.

From the very start, all the baby doctor wanted to talk about was how breastfeeding your new baby was the best choice.

Convinced, Dana switched from bottles to breast before it was too late and her milk had gone south.

Then, soon after Baby Kaitlin's weight plummeted, the same doctor had treated her like she was an unfit mother, with her too short, too skinny baby.

Dana changed doctors and stocked up on formula. When Kaitlin had graduated from the WHO charts to CDC growth charts, Dana no longer permitted anyone to measure her baby.

She was a *baby*, not a map. She did not care to know the 'longitude' of her infant.

Therapist Gert had told her she had made a major personal breakthrough by admitting to herself a few days ago, how frustrated she was about her daughter's height. Or lack thereof. Gert had her shout: "I HATE MY LIFE!" fifteen times at last week's session to expel some of her resentment. It had helped quite a bit.

Hormone treatments would cost roughly $35,000 an inch, but thankfully, money was not a problem.

If that Mother Nature bitch was not going to waive her growth spurt wand, then Mother Dana was going to waive hers.

She knew her daughter would not be able to cope if the other team members kept growing and she did not. It might very well signal the end to her daughter's place on her elite World Championship U-13 8-Hand Céilí A Team next year.

Attaching a large hair donut under Kaitlin's wig had given her another few important inches and had fixed the 'obviously way too short' problem for now, but she could not continue extending her daughter's height by propping it up with a prosthetic device under synthetic hair. Kaitlin would end up looking like Marge Simpson if she kept on elevating her wig like this.

Not on my watch, Dana thought, impatiently looking at her outdated Rolex before she remembered that this watch no longer worked and was now only worn as a very expensive diamond bracelet.

She flipped her mobile open. Just as she suspected, she had been waiting here to speak with doctor *what's her name* and her magic panel for over twenty minutes.

Today was the final interview to discuss Kaitlin's growth plan. She needed to grow at least three more inches if she were going to be chosen again to go to the Worlds next year with the A Team in her own age group. She would never be able to move down, even if she were shorter than the younger dancers, because the Irish dancing rule that older dancers could never move *down* for team dancing but younger ones could

8

move *up*, was strictly enforced. Like that made sense.

Her daughter was totally trapped in her short body with nowhere to go unless her mother intervened.

At the rate her daughter was *not* growing now, next year's céilí team dancing would never happen since, although unspoken, everyone had to be approximately the same size on a team or it ruined the 'look.'

I actually do get that, she had begrudgingly admitted to herself and Therapist Gert.

Kaitlin's Irish dance teachers would be delighted if they would have a legitimate reason to get rid of her short daughter along with her short mother.

Dana was also desperate to put an end to the awful nightmares she had been having lately. She could not remember the last time that she had gone to bed and awakened the next morning feeling refreshed.

The dream was always the same. It began with her DD standing on a competition stage in a circle with the other team dancers, arms stiffly down at her side, waiting for the cue to raise them up and clasp hands with the dancers on both sides of her.

Except that in this dream, when her little girl lifted her arms, they only reached up as far as the elbows of the dancers on either side of her.

Flailing like a baby bird falling out of its nest, her daughter desperately jumped up over and over, trying to grab on to the hands next to her—but she could not reach them.

She was too short.

Instead, the fickle team dancers always found the

anxious hands of one of the Subs. It was never clear in her dream whether it was Sub #1 or Sub #2 who had replaced her daughter Kaitlin and ruined her life.

The dream would continue until the taller dancers closed the circle in front of her daughter and began their 8-hand céilí dance while Kaitlin, standing outside the circle, sobbing inconsolably, watched them fly by.

Over my dead body....

"Is there a Dana waiting?" a friendly woman called out from the reception desk.

She smiled when Dana stood up and directed her to the Authorized door, where a nurse in blue scrubs was waiting to present the next parent to the verdict panel of hormone-injectors.

It occurred to Dana, that perhaps she should have brought her lawyer along to argue on her behalf if the medical decision turned out not to be a rousing, "Yes! Yes! Let's move ahead and do this growing!"

Or, perhaps Gert should have come along today to enable her to get through this ordeal.

As she followed the chatty nurse, Dana considered now whether or not she should have told her husband, Kaitlin's father, about the hormone shots.

Maybe. Maybe not. He had a tendency to overreact to things she told him.

She also wondered whether or not she should have married a taller man.

Introducing Brandi

$\mathcal{B}$randi made it her hobby to deliberately wreak havoc on the Voy Forums Irish Dance Message Boards. She concentrated on the regions where her daughter's 4-hand céilí team was scheduled to compete at feiseanna throughout the year.

She would begin by carefully analyzing the schools coming to these competitions which had dancers who were serious rivals of her daughter, Katelynne, in her Prizewinner level Treble Jig. Most of these solo steps competitors were also on a Brandi-targeted céilí team.

At first, Brandi had done her Voying around mostly just for fun, but she had discovered over the years how gratifying it was when she successfully unnerved other dancers' mothers. Better than a large banana split with whipped cream, nuts, and maraschino cherries, if she could tell that she had succeeded in driving the Voyers into a frenzied state of mind with her put-downs. She liked to imagine them pulling their hair out in large clumps.

During the feiseanna she had 'worked,' she studied the Voyers' DDs for signs of not 'taking charge' of their steps. Not 'owning' them as TCs put it. She liked to think that perhaps the dancers from other schools looked uncomfortable due to her efforts.

If she had successfully engaged with their mothers beforehand by launching efficient, anonymous insult grenades during the two weeks preceding a feis, it was their rattled mothers' fault if their DDs did not 'own' their steps on competition stages.

Brandi had never outgrown girl fights.

Her *modus operandi* was to harass only those Voyers who had taken their 'final vows' on the forums—the ones who had promised to faithfully cause trouble by scalding others' egos and wounding fragile feelings.

She had perfected her Voy attacks over the years. The trick to it, was simply to start a small brush fire at the right moment—not too long before targeted Irish dance competitions, but long enough beforehand to watch the front-line infantry of the Message Boards begin to leak negativity like a bad oil spill.

Brandi was not sure what she enjoyed most about being an experienced MAID—watching her talented daughter Katelynne 'owning' her competition stages, or fencing with the short-fused, mean-spirited Voyers during the weeks leading up to Irish dancing events.

Introducing Sylvia

"*I* know who wrote it," Sylvia announced gleefully at The Table. The music started up simultaneously in the practice room on what would soon prove to be the last normal Thursday night before the Worlds.

The MAIDS sitting at The Table glanced up from their reading materials.

"I know who wrote that letter." Reading materials were quickly discarded as all eyes became riveted on the speaker.

The smile of satisfaction on Sylvia's face reminded Sarah of her cat, Tabitha, purring and licking her paws.

13

It was generally known around the school that only The Top Tier Table MAIDS had been made privy to reading the malignant, unsigned letter sent to their T.C.R.G. last week.

It was also known that the Top Tier Table MAIDS were uniformly tight-lipped and very unlikely to break under any pressure, because they had promised their T.C.R.G. to remain silent, and to help her expose the Letter-Writer. Covertly of course, like double agents.

Sylvia, being only the mother of Sub #1 and thus not a real mother of one of the A Team dancers, had not been permitted to read the letter.

"How ever did you find out?" Brandi asked eagerly.

The MAIDS, practically panting with anticipation, begged Sylvia to explain.

Sylvia, savoring the moment, paused for dramatic effect, toying with the MAIDS, who reminded her of a pack of baying scent hounds on a long leash.

"I got a vibe in the bathroom while I was washing my hands at the sink when—and I shall call her 'Lady X,'—walked in. Acting on my gut feeling, I just asked her why she wrote it," she said offhandedly, like a psychic who routinely solved baffling mysteries in bathrooms.

Sylvia was elated to see obvious signs of approval at the MAIDS' Table. This was the first time she was sure that these women were actually listening to what she was saying. Normally, she was totally ignored—except for Sarah, who was always nice to her. Sarah was nice to everybody.

"Naturally, at first she looked very uncomfortable," Sylvia continued.

"But when I said I thought her letter was brilliant, she opened up like a morning glory. I *am* an attorney, you know. I learned how to question suspects during my mock trial in law school long before I got my law degree."

The instant recognition, perhaps even respect, that Sylvia had garnered from the school's Top Tier dance mothers with this startling information, fueled Sylvia's presentation, elevating it to a performance level. She was, for the first time ever, center stage, sitting at The Table with the Queen Bee MAIDS.

"I honestly don't blame her for not signing it," she said. Then she went on, as if addressing a jury: "Would any of *you* have signed that letter?" She lifted her fuzzy eyebrows questioningly, challenging the MAIDS to be honest with themselves.

Sighs and shrugs followed this probing inquiry.

"Well then, I say the 'Noes' have it!" Sylvia laughed, shrilly.

"Please correct me if I am wrong here, 'Attorney' Sylvia, but *you* did not read that letter," Jessica pointed out, wearing a nasty smirk on her pinched face.

"As I recall, you were asked to *leave* The Table when I shared the letter with the A Team mothers."

Melissa wondered whether or not Jessica really was as mean-spirited as she often appeared to be.

"Only eight of us have read that unfortunate letter as far as I am aware," Jessica sneered condescendingly, concluding her harsh closing argument as she searched Sylvia's face for signs of being humiliated, or perhaps a hint of flustered acknowledgement.

"I would not have signed that letter either," Sylvia plowed on, smiling slyly, pointedly ignoring Jessica's biting comment, "but I think I speak for everyone here at The Table when I say that none of us should ever speak to that bitch again. She's trouble."

Sylvia's referring to the unknown letter writer as a "bitch," was unsettling. She hardly ever talked at The Table except for spewing unsolicited advice. Hearing her use the 'B' word, made the MAIDS feel somewhat uncomfortable. It was obvious to the MAIDS that she was desperately trying to fit in.

Sylvia instantly regretted having introduced the 'B' word into her summation and also the shunning idea. The Letter-Writer deserved better. She seemed like a nice, unpretentious lady. *At least the Queen Bees normally shunned all of The Others anyway,* Sylvia consoled herself.

"So **who** is it then?" demanded Jessica. "How are we supposed to shun the 'bitch' who wrote that letter, if we don't know WHO she is?" *Like this wretched Sylvia woman is going to tell US how to respond?*

The muffled giggles from the MAIDs at The Table, greatly irritated Sylvia when she realized it really would be impossible for the inner circle to shun the Letter-Writer if she did not reveal who the Letter-Writer was.

She had obviously not been prepared to make this dramatic presentation tonight. She should have waited for a bit—thought it through better.

Sylvia's DD, Caytlin, had told her that most of the older dancers in the school knew all about the Letter-Writer and were trying to figure out who would have done such a 'Mean Girls-Burn Book' kind of thing to their wonderful T.C.R.G.

Sylvia hoped that the fact she knew who the Letter-Writer was, but was not going to tell anyone, would not embarrass her DD. She even dared to hope that her daughter would think that her mousy mother had suddenly become interesting and mysterious. The last thing on earth Sylvia wanted to do was to embarrass Caytlin.

"I am afraid that I am not at liberty to say," Sylvia replied to the scornful faces around her. "I promised her I wouldn't say anything."

The hostile, *you cannot be serious looks,* were followed by indignant exclamations of, "So? You are seriously *not* going to tell us? You're the bitch!"

The MAIDS' noses wrinkled up and their nostrils flared, highlighting their collective disgust.

"Nope," Sylvia flippantly replied, scrambling for a shred of dignity, but thoroughly pleased with herself for not sucking up to The Table at such a critical point in her relationship with these A Team MAIDS headed to the World Championships. Knowledge was power.

"It was a private conversation. I shouldn't have said that I found out who it was—that was careless of me and I apologize."

"I really can't explain why I told all of you in the first place. I should not have done that. I just thought

17

that you might be somewhat interested that the author had owned up to writing the letter and has no regrets."

Sylvia smiled tentatively, hopeful eyes darting from face to face. No one smiled back at her except Sarah, who had the courage to flash a thumbs up.

Even though it was an honor being the mother of the #1 Sub of a céilí team heading to the Worlds, the odds were that Sylvia's daughter, Caytlin, was not really going to be subbed in and everyone at The Table knew it, as did she.

This inevitability meant that the MAIDS had never extended a warm welcome to her. Why should they?

She and her daughter were only temporary.

The real A Team dancers might, and their mothers certainly *would,* do almost anything to hold on to their DD's rightful place. A DD being totally immobilized would probably be the only acceptable criteria before Caytlin would be given the go-ahead. Even then…

The reality was, Sylvia and her hard-working DD, would go off to the Worlds feeling guilty about hoping that Caytlin would have the chance to perform on the A Team. Because that would mean that another dancer was out of commission.

Sylvia wondered how many of the MAIDS would resort to cortisone shots and two cans of Red Bull and snorting Pixie Stix powder and whatever else it might take to get their DD's body up on stage to prevent a Sub from butting in.

Introducing Valerie

*V*alerie admired the sparkling turquoise water below. It reminded her of how the Swarovski crystals on her daughter's current solo dress twinkled, if stage lights had been fitted with blue gels.

It was exciting that she and her DD, Catelin, were traveling to a place where Catelin would be able to tan naturally in March, long before it would be possible at their country club's outside pool.

She fondly remembered tanning on lovely summer afternoons. When she had been on the pageant circuit in Alaska, she had always managed, at least from May through July, to find the sun's natural rays.

It had always paid off. Unlike many other wannabe

crowned beauty queens, *she* had never looked like she had applied the wrong Cover Girl foundation and left her hairline exposed, like a forgotten white headband.

Authentic bronze skin tones would call attention to Catelin's well-developed calf muscles when she did her quivers and leapovers, and might also make her stand out among the fake-tanned members of her céilí team. Like she used to stand out herself in her pageant days.

She was proud that she had never once resorted to fake tanning. A few times, she had been too broke to pay for enough fuel to drive to a sunny location, but she had placed first in those pageants, even with her snow-white skin.

It was fairly accurate to say, that she had sometimes envied her competitors who had naturally darker skin tones, but she had always tried to make the best of the skin color that she had been born with.

The operative word was always, 'natural.' If she had been able to naturally darken her exquisite, porcelain-white skin by tanning outside, so much the better. But she had *never*, and her daughter would *never*, no matter how much she begged, be permitted to artificially tan her body. An authentic tan was never a problem from mid-spring into mid-autumn. It was only during the dreary winter months that her DD's skin lost its amber edge. Valerie had never subscribed to that propaganda about global warming. The warmer the better. Alaska had been far too cold.

How could *natural* rays from the *natural* sun cause skin cancer? That was just crazy.

20

The expressions on the harpies' faces at The Table, when they saw that her Catelin was not painted naval orange or copper penny like their own overly indulged DDs, would be priceless.

Before drifting off, she envisioned Catelin in her new solo dress—the one that would complement her spectacular natural tan-to-be. Which colors would best enhance a natural tan? Probably white but then again, perhaps a pale yellow. A creamy yellow...

An announcement from the flight deck interrupted her pleasant reverie. Why did she need to be told they were going to land soon? Who cared?

She closed her tired eyes again. It was wonderful that Irish dancers often wore wigs, because she could easily change her daughter's naturally light brown hair color, if she thought another color would better suit her solo dress.

So many mothers missed the wig-dress relationship and bought the solo dress without considering the wig color that would best tie the whole look together.

She would call solo dress designers as soon as they returned from vacation. Easter was coming up and so was the Worlds. She could easily afford to double any designer's fees, and was confident that she could get exactly what she wanted, when she wanted it—if she could only decide what it *was* that she wanted.

The resort hotel had been briefed as to her dietary concerns about her daughter's tendency to crave and then sneakily order buckets of greasy food when the coast was clear.

Catelin had done careless Room Service ordering before. Didn't she realize her forbidden food would be itemized on their final check out bill?

But then, Catelin obviously knew she would not get into much, if any trouble, for her out-of-control eating episodes. She had always been 'Daddy's Little Girl' and could do no wrong. Ever.

At this resort, there would be no discussion about what her DD would be ordering from Room Service.

They had already been instructed as to what kinds of food were not allowed to be ordered from Room 209.

Menus had been discussed and modified to include food that a dedicated Irish dancer could confidently choose. Food that would not compromise her weight while boosting her energy level.

Housekeeping had assured Valerie that the altered Room 209 menu would be in place when they arrived at their suite.

Valerie had resisted telling Catelin the exciting news about 'Ann,' the Irish dance coach she had retained to whip her daughter into optimum shape for solos at the Worlds.

Maybe she would tell her about Ann during the ride to the resort. Maybe just wait until Ann actually turned up. It was very important not to give her daughter the opportunity to object and thereby cause an argument.

Valerie already had more than enough arguing with her husband and tried to avoid ugly mother-daughter confrontations whenever possible.

Annoying wind noise created by the landing gear being lowered jolted her back to being fully conscious. Which Mexican resort had she booked? Was it Playa del Carmen, Cancun?

Resorts were basically all the same, no matter what country they happened to be in.

Maybe the arrival airport's name would be posted and reveal their location. It really didn't matter because the resort's limo driver would have a sign welcoming them and then take them to wherever it was that they were going.

If she needed to, she knew she could always find it on her mobile somewhere. And as a last resort, pop some pills, call her husband, and let him figure it out. She probably should tell him anyway why the two of them were not going to be home for the next ten days.

The man would miss having his beautiful daughter at dinner each night, asking her how her day had been and actually listening to his baby girl's conversation.

Valerie could not remember when her husband had asked *her* how *her* day had gone, or anything else about her pathetic life for that matter.

It seemed to Valerie that, after she had packed away her pageant tiaras and given her twenty-five evening gowns to the local high school for girls who could not afford a prom dress, her life had been basically over.

After Catelin had been born, it was official.

She was a has-been.

Giving birth to any more children would have been far too painful for her to endure—after their births.

She had traded in her meaningless fertility to maintain the little sanity she still possessed.

Valerie was looking forward to meeting Ann.

She had done background checks and fact-finding, prior to engaging the twenty-year-old, former World Champion.

She had been delighted when Ann had accepted her offer. It was a lot of money, but she was confident that Ann would be well worth it.

Valerie did not mention to Ann, or her daughter, that tanning and getting Catelin ready for the Worlds, were not the only reasons they were traveling to Mexico for ten days.

Valerie was going to undergo a 'neck lift' to put an end to the sagging skin that made it unbearable to be seen in public without a silk scarf in warm weather and turtleneck sweater when it was cooler.

She was far too pretty to have a saggy neck.

Next year, she might have her nose shortened, or maybe the bags under her eyes removed. She had been blessed with big green eyes, and with a shorter nose, they would appear even bigger. She would do the nose next year.

Other than working with Catelin on her solo steps, she demanded only that Ann supervise her daughter's tanning each day, and make sure that she faithfully ran her daily mile.

Introducing Michelle

*W*hen the trusted family doctor told Michelle and her DD, Katelyn, that he would not inject Katelyn's right knee with another cortisone shot to ease the pain she endured when she danced, Michelle lost her external calm demeanor.

Regrouping, she tugged nervously at her curly, dark brown hair and said:

"I don't think you *understand*, Doctor. She is going to go to the World Irish Dance Championships!"

"**The Worlds!**" She resisted making a big round circle with her arms to illustrate her point.

"You see, her dance céilí team actually qualified and

Katelyn is a very important component of that team. She can neither let herself, nor her team down, just because she has this temporary knee problem."

"You and I both know that this is not a 'temporary' problem, Michelle," Doctor Horan said patiently in his middle-aged-tired, but genuinely concerned voice.

"Katelyn has had the same chronic knee problems on and off for three years now. I have told you several times that she needs to take a break from dancing so she can heal properly."

"But it's only some tendonitis, Doctor. You know that Katelyn has flare ups from time to time. This time she needs one shot so she can continue practicing with her céilí team, and then just one more for the World Championships in a few weeks. After Easter, it will all be over. She will have her first gold medal from the Worlds and I promise you, we will take a long hiatus from Irish dancing and monitor Katelyn's progress. We will start physical therapy and…"

Doctor Horan, his brown eyes uncharacteristically flashing, interrupted.

"You know exactly what's going on here, Michelle. I have always been totally upfront with you."

"Katelyn," Doctor Horan said, "please go out to the reception area and have a snack. There should be some muffins left. I need to talk with your mother privately for a bit. We won't be long."

Katelyn nodded and smiled pleasantly, hoping that Doctor Horan would forbid her to continue dancing until the pain went away for good, even if he did give her another cortisone shot now. She could tell he cared about her. Why else would he have asked her to leave his examination room? The cortisone shots had always been a disappointment. When she would begin to be pain free and feel normal again, the pain would slowly return, until she needed another one.

The shots always wore off.

Since her mother would not permit her to use pain killers like Tylenol because they were "harmful in large amounts—especially to children"—if she was not able to get an injection today, she did not know what she would do. It was her only option. She was desperate.

She might have to totally freak her mom out and go stay with her dad. He at least let her take Tylenol. All her mom ever did was hand her an ice pack. When it melted, she would give her another one. Always icing her knee, so she would not damage her stomach with pain killers.

Doctor Horan could see that Michelle was ready to explode. He had urged her to seek help for the obvious depression which had swallowed her up like a thick morning fog, ever since her husband had moved out.

So far, she had not heeded his medical advice for herself, or for her daughter's chronic knee problems, and he feared today's refusal might send her over the edge. He had watched Michelle age ten years since her ex-husband had moved in with a graduate student at his university. With this in mind, he proceeded carefully.

"Michelle, you know there have been some minor

arthritic changes to your daughter's kneecap and the tendonitis is recurring because Katelyn aggravates her delicate condition every time she dances. It has got to *stop*—at *least* for the time being, Michelle, until Katelyn has time to recover completely. A cortisone shot will only mask the pain and her precarious condition will continue to worsen. Her tendons will soon be like an old woman's the way this is heading."

"Is that what you want? A child who has created an unnecessary physical impairment all by herself before she is even thirteen years old?"

"I am truly sorry, Michelle, but with a long hiatus and some good physical therapy, Katelyn can heal and continue dancing. But she needs to stop *now* and we'll see how she feels next fall."

"In the meantime, give her Tylenol. But you must STOP the dancing—no world championships. After the break, she should be good to go again next fall."

Next fall my ass...!

Michelle could see clearly that this pathetic old man was not going to treat her daughter's pain.

She left the office, collected Katelyn, grabbed her own muffin and huffed out to the parking lot.

Michelle reported that Doctor Horan could not do another cortisone shot, but he had suggested another clinic that *would* do the shot and had given her some sample Tylenol for now.

Katelyn permitted herself to dare to hope that her mother would allow her Tylenol before her next shot. If not, she would be moving in with her father.

Introducing Stacey

"*Y*ou will feel so much better if you can just throw it up, L'il Darlin," Stacey cooed in her buttery Southern drawl. She smiled encouragingly and passed the blue heirloom chamber pot to her daughter, Caitlyn.

After Caitlyn had completely emptied her stomach, Stacey suggested that they watch an old episode of Dance Moms together.

Caitlyn, annoyed, but not wanting to disappoint her demanding mother, agreed, even though she thought that show was not worth anyone's time. Especially her own.

She put her new mystery book down on the coffee table and sipped the Diet 7-Up her mother had given her to replace lost fluids.

Her mom was right again. She did feel better now

that she had vomited.

Caitlyn had not been feeling well lately, but Stacey was encouraged, because Doctor Crystal thought her DD was looking better—even though she had actually gained back three of the fifteen pounds she had lost over the past six months.

Stacey was optimistic about her daughter's progress too, but for another reason. Her daughter had reached an important milestone.

She had become comfortable with eliminating the contents of her stomach, before digestion started up full throttle.

If I keep her on the high protein, low carb diet and she gets one hour of aerobic exercise in each day, she will stabilize. No sugar. No fats. Mega vitamins. She is not going to blimp out like I have. She needs to lose those three pounds she gained back....

Stacey firmly believed that vomiting should be the absolute last recourse to weight loss. Resorted to only when, like minutes ago, chocolate candy bar wrappers had been discovered, along with some empty potato chip bags, hidden in the bottom of Caitlyn's backpack.

It was obvious Caitlyn was aware that she was being spied upon, since she always left the hardcore evidence in her backpack.

So why *did* she *hide* the evidence and not carefully discard it before she returned home?

Obviously because she wants to be caught, Stacey thought,

pleased with her psychoanalytical abilities. Sometimes psyching your daughter out was incredibly easy.

Stacey was proud of her daughter for not littering the earth. Pretending to hide her used candy wrappers for her mother to discover was the better, more moral thing to do. The environmentally friendly choice.

Stacey had, over the years, instilled in her daughter a sense of responsibility as to the choices one needed to make after indulging in the sin of gluttony.

"Before the bodily consequences of digesting junk food can take hold of you, creating slimy layers of lumpy, white fat, the fats and sugar overloads must be immediately dealt with by purging."

Bodily waste was easily disposed of by vomiting and regularly using laxatives, but non-biodegradable junk and oceans full of toxic nuclear waste and plastic six-pack holders and dead birds that had choked on cheap balloons that careless parents had released at birthday parties year after year....

Mother Earth could not tolerate much more abuse.

The simple facts were, God had given the human race a paradise and look what had become of it.

It was enough to make someone crazy.

Even though she disagreed with Doctor Crystal's being overly-concerned about how thin her daughter had become, she had listened politely at Caitlyn's last office checkup, as the frumpy physician had cautioned her about Caitlyn's drastic weight loss.

Annoyed with Dr. Crystal's hesitancy about taking so long to get to her real point, she had lied when the nosy physician began probing around, asking personal questions.

Just go right ahead and ask me, Doctor.

Is she bulimic or anorexic?

And I will tell YOU that it's none of your business.

So butt out!

Take a good look at yourself, why don't you?

Because, Doctor Crystal, if the truth be told, you could stand to lose some weight yourself!

Introducing Sarah

Sarah, like her daughter, Caitlin, had started to think that Irish dancing was not so much fun anymore. It seemed that lately one, or both of them, was stressing out about something directly related to it.

There were the often, but not unexpected, minor physical complaints that her daughter endured without complaining. However, there were also indications of considerable mental stress presenting in both of them.

Caitlin was constantly trying to balance her dancing with homework and friends and practicing every day in the basement on the stage her father had built for her years ago.

Volleyball, which she had always enjoyed, was not possible because half of the games were out of town and the team's bus sometimes got back as late as 8:00 p.m. Same for basketball. Same for swim team.

There was also not being able to go on winter ski trips after school because they interfered with her Irish dancing classes, not being able to go to sleepovers, or have them herself on Saturday nights, because she had to dance two or more days a week and one practice was always on Sunday at noon.

She could not afford staying up all night watching movies and talking, if she were going to be in proper condition to execute her Open Championship dance steps in front of her T.C.R.G. early the next day.

Everything in their family's holiday life seemed to revolve around Irish dancing—Thanksgiving, the 4th of July and now Easter again this year—since Caitlin's team had qualified for the Worlds and she had also, for the third time, qualified to do her solo steps.

Thankfully, Sarah's twenty-year-old son was always off at college or on a summer internship somewhere. If he did still live at home fulltime, he would think she was having a serious midlife crisis, constantly yielding to the demands Irish dancing presented while working full time as a pharmacist.

Sarah had also noticed lately that the pharmacist's job she had always loved was becoming burdensome. She lacked her old energy level, and hoped that when the Worlds was over with she would bounce back to her normal, energetic self again.

She often reflected about how this obsessive Irish dancing vocation had begun. She had taken Caitlin to a touring production of *Riverdance* five years ago. It was during that show that both of their fates had been sealed.

While Sarah had an Irish genetic package, Caitlin's father was mostly German and Norwegian, with a bit of Welsh. His genes, however, had not been sufficient to do battle with the obsession that their daughter had suddenly developed to become an Irish dancer.

Sarah had come to think it had been like some kind of life-changing, religious conversion experience, for both daughter and mother. An epiphany of some sort.

She now feared that *she* was the one who had been enabling the almost fanatical lifestyle both mother and daughter had shared for five years. By encouraging her daughter to forego regular Middle School activities, and prioritizing Irish dancing above all else, she had become the classic 'stage mother.'

She was the mom, so why couldn't she figure it all out? Or just stop it? She was beginning to feel like she was riding on a rollercoaster with too many dips.

At least Caitlin liked many of the girls in her dance school. Sarah wished that she could say the same thing about liking their mothers.

The younger, trendier moms, usually wore designer jeans that highlighted their firm fannies, and tight tops that stretched across their firm breasts. Sarah thought of them as 'urban women with cave-women depth.'

She thought of herself as being on a slow descent to becoming middle-aged.

The older, droopier mothers like herself seemed to be as self-absorbed as the fashionistas, but often they were even more draining, tending to talk passionately about whatever subject it was at the moment that most interested them—as long as it was about Irish dancing.

During many conversations at the U-13 8-Hand Céilí A Team Table, Sarah felt like she was trapped on an Irish Dance Pinterest Board, unable to find her mouse and click off.

She was afraid she might go crazy if she heard one more MAID use the 'A' letter when referencing their DDs' céilí team. She intended to tell all of the MAIDS, when she thought that the time was right, that since there was not a U-13 'B' team at their dance school, it made no sense referring to their DDs as the 'A' Team.

Even though Sarah tolerated the MAIDS, she had seriously considered going off to read a book during dance classes.

To escape from the relentless demands of being a competitive championship Irish dancer, Sarah and her daughter often visited the Public Museum's Butterfly Room for much-needed infusions of serenity.

If a butterfly would land on an outstretched hand, it felt like being brushed by a grace from heaven.

Introducing Linda

$\mathcal{L}$inda was running fifteen minutes late because of a fender bender blocking the entire left lane and Kaetlin needed to be at her swim team practice in ten minutes which was now impossible.

This was a major crisis.

She knew her daughter would be a case of nerves by now waiting in front of school. *I should have let her father pick her up. He's closer to the school but he is not reliable.*

Linda had realized long ago that her partner's idea of time management was leaving for a meeting at the office or an important event, with only a few minutes of wiggle room for traffic.

Since GPS had arrived, he now allowed even less time, and Kaetlin knew this. It had caused her so much distress that one time, after he was ten minutes late, she had to be driven directly to the Emergency Room to deal with an immobilizing headache.

Another time, Linda had received a costly speeding ticket after responding to a frantic call from Kaetlin asking, "Exactly where are you right now and what is your best ETA?"

Both parents had finally forbidden her to call just to check up on them. So far, Kaetlin had respected this ultimatum, even though she was often red-faced when her parents arrived a minute or so late.

It was obvious to both MAID and father, that their daughter was a mess, but so far, neither of them had been able to think of a way to calm Kaetlin down. She was like a taut violin string all the time, but if someone was not exactly on time picking her up for an activity, she more or less had a nervous breakdown.

Linda called her daughter on the car's remote and explained that she was going to be late because of the left lane problem.

"You know that the first half hour is warmup laps, Kaetlin. I'll just explain what happened. It's not your fault."

The silence on the other end was deafening.

Finally, a tiny squeak, no louder than a drip from a faucet replied, "Okay."

Why didn't I allow more time? Linda groaned, shifting into fifth gear, checking her side and rearview mirrors for speed traps.

As she raced to pick up her daughter, she thought about the possibility of asking Kaetlin whether or not she enjoyed doing so many activities.

Irish dancing was her DD's top priority, but maybe gymnastics, swim team, piano lessons and soccer was pushing things a bit?

There was rarely ever a free moment for Kaetlin or herself. If Kaetlin were not an only child, this rat race would be impossible. She sometimes wondered if her daughter, who seemed to take everything for granted, had ever thought about that.

As things were now, Linda could not remember the last time she had her hair done or had even 'done' it herself. There was never any time in between her two jobs—engineer and organizer of Kaetlin's activities.

She noticed that she had started putting on weight recently, allowing herself to eat drive-through comfort food while she waited for her daughter to be finished with one activity and driven on to the next.

Her home cooking had degenerated into large trays of frozen lasagna and many other family-sized frozen casseroles, containing so much sodium they tasted like natural salt deposits.

She tried to remember to include fresh vegetables with her thrown-together meals, but preparing them took too much energy, so she usually opted for frozen greens. If she remembered to buy them.

Perhaps it was time to ask Kaetlin if she would like to drop gymnastics. Although Linda had recently read that Irish dancing was becoming very athletic.

No. Not gymnastics. What if future céilí team steps included back flips or triple cartwheels?

Perhaps Kaetlin could give up the city swim team?

No. Bad idea because swimming was improving Kaetlin's endurance. Definitely making her Hornpipe less of a breathing problem.

Perhaps piano could go? It was stressful getting her daughter to practice.

No. Not piano. Piano was definitely improving Kaetlin's sense of timing and rhythm.

Soccer would have to go.

Kaetlin's knees are starting to look like they belong on a 9-year-old boy.

It might be more beneficial for her daughter to take up mixed martial arts for stress relief. Or perhaps, even better, yoga at the local Y.M.C.A.

Sometimes, Linda thought that she might be over-scheduling her DD, but as she knew well from her own experience, if one was going to excel at everything like she had at Vassar and then at Dartmouth, you had to become disciplined about managing your time.

In the long run, she was giving her daughter a jump start to handling the many time crunches a busy life presented. Linda was adamant that her DD was going to follow in her mother's capable footsteps.

She had, in fact, devoted her entire life to this end.

Introducing Melissa

𝒯idal waves of dread engulfed Melissa, waking her up again for the fifth night in a row. This meant, that the three hours of fitful sleeping she had already endured, might be it for the night.

It was time to invite 'Insomnia,' the evil twin sister of 'Nightmare,' to join her for yet another final round of nightcaps.

Melissa's irresponsible binge-drinking started soon after it had become obvious that her DD, Keightlinne, had grown out of her pink solo dress. Therefore, her DD had no solo dress to wear at the Worlds because

Melissa had also discovered that there were no funds available in the household budget to buy her another one. To say that this was unfair was an understatement.

Dana was going to pump growth hormones into *her* daughter. *I should have such a problem. My daughter is growing faster than the weeds in our backyard,* she thought.

Unlike Dana, who had more money than she knew how to spend, Melissa had almost no money to spend on anything other than the bare necessities when her beloved school system laid off fifty teachers. She had been the forty-ninth casualty.

Melissa found the half-empty bottle of cheap vodka she had hidden in the upstairs bathroom's toilet water box and took care not to slam the lid as she closed it.

She crept down the old wooden stairs, avoiding the squeaky areas. Not taking the risk of switching on the overhead hall light, she slowly made her way through the darkened family room until she finally reached the sanctuary that her comfortable kitchen provided.

She removed the Sleepy Time mug with the Three Bears and Goldilocks from its mug tree, and sat down at her grandmother's old farmhouse table.

At first, she had mixed Diet 7-Up with the vodka when she would binge. Now, she just sipped it straight. No point in wasting good 7-Up.

In an hour or so, she would hopefully be looped enough to go back to bed, pass out, and get in a few more hours before the 7:00 a.m. alarm went off.

She did not have to worry about still being legally drunk, or very hungover in the mornings, because her husband drove the girls to school every day and she always sobered up by the time her family returned. She never started the drinking until everyone else had gone to bed, and she slept in most mornings.

The era of Melissa's having been able to get a good night's sleep, had abruptly ended when she discovered that she had dug herself into a hole so deep, it would be next to impossible to climb out.

She would try the slots again today while the girls were at their after-school activities and her husband was working late. The shuttle to the casino was only a few blocks away.

What had she been thinking? Obviously she had *not* been thinking.

Why had she ever thought, drunk or sober, that her daughter, Keightlinne, needed ***three*** new solo dresses for the upcoming World Championships?

A Monet-inspired 'Poppy Fields' dress for her Slip Jig, a bold Carmen 'Habanera' red dress for her Treble Jig and a gorgeous, shimmery black spider dress for her recall.

What if her daughter did not get a recall? She decided to hide the black dress until it was needed, just in case.

They were, after all, dancing at the Worlds, where every dancer would probably be at least as good, if not better than her own daughter. Being very realistic, it was entirely possible that Keightlinne might not get a recall.

Keightlinne had been positively saint-like after she realized that her lovely pink satin solo dress no longer fit and there was no money for a new one.

She had suggested that perhaps they could swap her too small pink solo dress for one that would fit, that she was a competent dancer and that's all that really mattered.

"Judges did not have the time or interest to react to dresses as they critiqued dancers," she had said.

None of Melissa's considerable efforts to locate a larger dress had produced acceptable results and time had been running out when the fatal dress binge had occurred.

One small consolation at the time, had been that the secondary resale market for the three new Irish dance one-of-a-kind solo dresses, should be good. Especially if a dress had only been worn once or twice.

But she soon discovered, what she could realistically expect to get would not come anywhere close to what she had unwittingly spent.

She would sell two dresses after the Worlds and let her daughter pick the one she wished to keep. Perhaps the black recall one would never be worn and could be sold as new.

Having been inexcusably inebriated when she had embarked on that dress-buying orgy, Melissa had also purchased three new wigs: a medium blonde one for Keightlinne's lovely Slip Jig, a bun wig to match her daughter's dark brown hair for her Treble Jig and a long, extra-curly black one for the recall showdown.

Melissa had always held the theory that Irish dance adjudicators had to be subconsciously influenced by colors, and that smart mothers knew how to select the most pleasing combinations.

Brandi passionately disagreed with Melissa's naïve idea that 'color harmonies' could actually influence a judge's perception of a dancer's ability. She had put an end to the 'colors do matter' conversation, when she revealed that "many of the adjudicators were color-blind robots," although she admitted that so far, she had no real evidence of this.

She did have one semi-convincing observation to bolster her robot hypothesis—the adjudicators never made eye-to-eye contact because they had not been programmed do so. Therefore, it was highly unlikely that they were already programmed to appreciate color harmonies.

The 'colors matter' debate had ended with Brandi's final point: "Putting aside the robotic possibility, how could adjudicators be influenced by certain *colors* when the bling on some dresses is often so blinding that Irish dancers look like part of the light show on Fremont Street in Las Vegas after dark?"

***

*M*elissa's catastrophic string of ill-fated events, had commenced when she paid for the three extravagant dresses and wigs, using three unexpected, unsolicited credit cards that she had 'providentially' received in the mail on the same day.

It had seemed at the time, in her 'condition,' like a confluence of stars and planets in the heavens—she had been 'pre-approved.' Three times.

After she had maxed out the three cards, she put them in a drawer and promptly forgot all about them, having apparently been in a drunken stupor as she was busily spending their providential credit limits.

Weeks later, she was startled to receive several e-mails from an Irish dance dress designer, with very specific questions about her choice of colors for the three dresses she had 'ordered'…?

Thinking that the designer had obviously contacted the wrong person, she had put off replying, intending to correct the error after she went grocery shopping.

When she returned, she opened the mailbox on the porch and saw that three of the envelopes were from credit card companies. She was very tired of receiving solicitations to sign up for more debt. She went inside and plopped the junk mail on the hallway table.

She had forgotten about the new throwaway mail, until she checked her e-mail again. She then sent a curt reply: "I think you've got the wrong person."

Wish I could afford just one new dress for the Worlds, she had ironically thought at the time.

Thank heaven her husband had been out of town when she had discovered what she had actually done, during what had to have been an alcoholic blackout of Homeric dimensions.

Upon her frantic request, the dress designer had e-mailed her receipts for the dresses, which included the exorbitant international shipping fees with the charges applied to three separate credit cards.

She had soon discovered that the mail she had put

on the hallway table from the credit card companies, had not contained new solicitations.

Instead, there had been three separate statements for three totally maxed out credit cards. Her despair had been overwhelming.

The upstairs vodka bottle was almost empty, so she found her backup, emergency bottle, in the downstairs water box before she permitted herself to think again about what had happened—what she had done!

Things had gone from very bad to *so* much worse after she had found out that she had paid for each of the dress purchases in British pounds sterling, not U.S. dollars.

The already way out of her price range $3,000 per dress, that she must *thought* she had spent for a single dress, had actually cost approximately $4,800. Each. A total of $14,400 for three temporary solo dresses.

Obviously, the difference between the U.S. dollar sign $ and a British pound sterling sign £ had not been detected by her blacked-out, alcohol saturated brain.

Fortunately, the three wigs had been paid for in U.S. dollars. Four hundred dollars for the three wigs. At least she had not ordered new poodle socks with real diamonds.

Melissa had chosen not to think about how much interest was accruing as she filled her Three Bears mug up with the last drops of last night's vodka. Lifting her cup, she toasted Insomnia, her new BFF.

Her best guess, was that this descent into hell had commenced at a neighbor's birthday party. She had not paid much attention to how much party wine she had consumed, as she was only blocks from home and had walked both ways.

She had continued her drinking at home. Everyone would have been asleep when she got back.

That she had also provided dress measurements to the designer, while smashed, was almost unbelievable. She had no idea how she had managed that without a measuring tape—and her DD's body.

When the dresses had been delivered, Melissa was very thankful that they had turned out to be not only stunning, but tasteful.

Melissa was broke, but there was some consolation in imagining how thrilled her daughter would be when she got the first two solo dresses. The third dress, if she somehow managed to get the recall, would be like winning the solo dress lottery.

It would be quite difficult to explain to Keightlinne, how her mom had come to buy these new solo dresses. How there had suddenly been enough money for not only one new dress, but two or possibly even three, if she recalled and danced a third time.

It was very unlikely that her daughter still believed in Fairy Godmothers, so she would have to come up with some other explanation.

She would check into Rehab right after the Worlds.

Introducing
The Letter-Writer

$\mathcal{T}$he timid author of the notorious letter had merely pointed out, that she thought her DD was not getting any one-on-one attention like the other dancers in her class were.

Her little DD, Kaitlinn, complained regularly that she did not know how to do the jig like everybody else in her class.

The anxious Letter-Writer had spied from afar one

night. She had been disheartened and dismayed to see that the two drillers, who were running the class, were very attentive to the other cute little dancers, while her own neglected DD stood in one place, twirling around like an out-of-control spinning top, until she was so dizzy, she could no longer stand up and fell down on to the hard floor. She did this over and over again.

That explained the bruising on her daughter's legs and arms that had mysteriously appeared over the last few weeks. Angry and concerned as she had been at the time to witness her little girl being neglected, she was relieved there was an explanation for the bruises. She had already scheduled an appointment with the family doctor to rule out a serious medical condition.

She was only six. The entire half hour went by with the teachers working with the other dancers. Neither of them spoke to, nor helped her little girl.

Being extremely shy, the Letter-Writer composed a letter to the T.C.R.G. and expressed her concerns.

The Letter-Writer was completely flabbergasted by the reaction her letter had caused. She had only stated that, in her humble opinion, there were favorites in the class and that her own DD was being totally neglected.

She had neither signed the letter nor identified the class she was complaining about because she did not want to name the drillers and get them into trouble.

She had only hoped that her letter might prompt the T.C.R.G. to investigate, and perhaps encourage her staff to pay equal attention to everyone.

How had this mildly critical letter triggered such an

explosive, furious response? She had not even brought up the bruises.

And why did the T.C.R.G., to whom the letter had been addressed, let so many *others* read it?

The next thought caused the Letter-Writer to feel like she was going to faint. She grabbed on to a nearby chair to steady herself.

Why had the T.C.R.G. not asked her to read the letter? Was *she* the main suspect? How *could* she be? The loud whispering she had heard in the hallways had revealed that only the Top Tier Table mothers had been invited to read the letter.

She managed to pull herself together again when she realized that, since no one in the entire school ever talked to her—neither dance mother nor teacher, she could not possibly be a suspect, because no one knew that she existed. How silly to worry about nothing. She was only an eavesdropper ghost.

The Letter-Writer would forever be thankful that she had had the foresight *not* to have signed that letter. Who knows what would have happened if she had?

If word had gotten out, her overly enthusiastic new publicist would likely have sent a short press release entitled: "Heartbroken Author," along with one of her all-time worst mother-daughter photos.

She knew that she needed to get away from this ridiculous toxic environment, but hesitated to take her daughter out of school immediately, because if she did, it might be assumed that it was because of the letter. But then, so what? No one at the school knew who she was.

When her little Kaitlinn had taken to Irish dancing, she had been thrilled. It was something she had never been able to do herself while she was growing up.

Trying another school would be the next logical step, with a note to herself that, if the mothers in the next one were even half as crazy as the ones here, that would be the end of Irish dancing.

She might find a ballet school that produced their own Nutcracker. If she and Kaitlinn regularly watched some of the hundreds of Nutcrackers available online, her little girl would soon be dreaming about being one of those cute little mice.

Ever since she had retained a prominent civil trial attorney to look out for her interests, if things took an unexpected turn, she felt much more confident.

Her intellectual property lawyer was not equipped to handle a defamation lawsuit, should one surface.

The Letter-Writer returned to editing her book. If this one was half as successful as her other three, she would soon be off to Italy with her widowed mother and six-year-old daughter.

There was an Irish dance school in Rome she had investigated, so Kaitlinn would be able to continue her lessons there should she wish to do so.

It was ironic that usually, if she were out in public and someone had recognized her, they would ask for an autograph or photo. At the Irish dance school, she was like a tiny grease spot on an old rug.

Four Weeks Before The World Irish Dance Championships

*T*ension was slowly mounting at the Thursday night non-Worlds-bound classes due to the teaching staff's preoccupation with the upcoming event.

The Others felt like their DDs did not matter, and that their hard-earned money was only being used to promote the Top Tier dancers.

Most of them thought their Parents' Booster Club dues only boosted the dancers who had been ordained early on to become champions.

It was maintained by many that these anointed little ones had begun their Irish dance lessons only a few weeks after they had learned how to walk.

The Others imagined that the Booster Club funds they had involuntarily contributed over the years, were used to finance lavish teacher parties with the Top Tier parents, and first class airfares to expensive vacation resorts in Central or perhaps South America. During the upcoming Worlds, there would likely be expensive, vintage champagne toasts, sipped in lavish hotel suites, paid for with Booster Club funds.

The possibilities were endless. However, the great majority of The Others paid their Booster Club dues, without an accounting, concerned about what might happen to their DDs if they did not.

***

$\mathcal{T}$ension was particularly conspicuous among those MAIDS who were waiting for their DDs to be finished with their Worlds' céilí team and solo steps practices.

The MAIDS' uneasiness was mostly related to the unknown identity of the Letter-Writer. How well their DDs were preparing for the biggest event in their lives had almost become secondary to some of the MAIDS, although they did not yet realize it.

Most Top Tier MAIDS were filled with righteous indignation and hardly ever talked about anything else. Conversation at The Table was more like a television 'News Flash!' running on a repeat headline loop.

Some of The Others, who had become indifferent, and a bit removed from the never-ending conversation as to the identity of the anonymous letter's author, had started to drop their DDs off before class, and after class, like a taxi, picked them up at the front door.

Speculation was endless about which one of The Others had written the letter. Not unexpectedly, The Others who chose not to sit inside the school building while they waited for their DDs, were at the top of the

MAIDS' considerable list of suspects.

Some of the more sensitive, introspective Others, acted suspiciously, fearing they might be suspects— even though they knew firsthand that they had not written the offensive letter.

Others of The Others blushed when they passed by one of the MAIDS sitting at The Table, knowing that they might well be at the very top of The Table's list of 'Persons of Great Interest,' due to their noticeable inconspicuousness.

When the eyes of the Tier One MAIDS bore into them, they felt vulnerable, 'presumed guilty' by reason of disassociation from The Table.

**

*I*n the bathroom confessional, Sylvia had impulsively asked the Letter-Writer if she happened to have a copy of the anonymous letter in her purse, never dreaming that she actually would.

The nervous author had willingly turned it over and asked Sylvia if, like the grapevine said, she was really an attorney. When Sylvia had smiled and confirmed that this was indeed a fact, the Letter-Writer took out her checkbook and asked Sylvia to represent her.

Sylvia had hesitated for a brief moment, reviewing her options. Should she ask for a retainer of $5,000 to "look into the case?"

She quickly activated her dormant lawyer brain and told the Letter-Writer that there might be a problem if this Irish dance academy discovered her identity and then filed a defamation lawsuit.

Sylvia was happy that she had wisely decided to pay her State Bar dues again this year to remain 'active' and had also faithfully kept up with her Continuing Legal Education Credits every two years.

She made a mental note to go over her law school torts class notes to freshen up on how defamation libel differed from defamation slander.

The letter she had read seemed pretty tame, but if she were going to ask for a big retainer, she needed to make the Letter-Writer's case look complicated, like a dangerous mine field which would require competent legal assistance to get through it in one piece.

She told the Letter-Writer that she would definitely need legal representation if the letter she had written ended up destroying the dance school's reputation.

The Letter-Writer looked stricken.

"*How* could my insignificant letter ruin this school's reputation?" she had asked incredulously.

Sylvia realized that she had no idea whatsoever how this scenario could ever really happen. She had hoped that she would have had the opportunity to do some research before she had to start making sweeping legal remarks.

Indeed, how could this simple little letter convince any attorney to file such a simpleminded lawsuit? How could anyone ever prove damages unless there would suddenly be a mass exodus from the school? Even if that did happen, proving a causal relationship seemed impossible. The letter was still harmless.

Allegiance pledged to any Irish dancing school was

fleeting. Mothers were always switching schools. The usual reason they changed schools, had to do mostly with the success that the dancers at the other area Irish dance schools were having, or *seemed* to be having.

Sylvia decided to keep things uncomplicated. She told the Letter-Writer that, "This is a complex issue and before I speak any more about it with you, I would like to do a bit of research."

Neither she, nor any trial lawyers she could think of offhand, would ever file a defamation lawsuit based solely on an anonymous letter criticizing the amount of personal attention being given to one dancer. And Sylvia knew that in a court of law, judges did impose sanctions from time to time if a lawyer tried to take up the court's time with obvious no-merit nonsense.

"What are the damages?" was the eternal question asked by lawyers in determining whether or not to take on a case involving defamation.

Since Sylvia was an attorney who could represent either side of a legal issue, even if she actually thought that this particular case *might* have some merit, which she was almost certain it did not, she realized that, if push came to shove, she could not legally represent this dance academy, because everybody in the school knew that she had interviewed the Letter-Writer in the bathroom. She was, like it or not, the 'attorney' and the Letter-Writer was the 'client' who had reached out to her for legal help.

She had decided to ask the Letter-Writer for a non-refundable retainer of $5,000, hoping that the Letter-

Writer would fire her and find a real lawyer if things got too complicated.

During the initial bathroom consultation, she had torn off a large paper towel from its plastic holder and had hastily composed a short Retainer Agreement. She was well aware that they might be interrupted at any moment when, as it had been in her own case, parents headed to the bathroom after they had consumed two cups of hot coffee.

Sylvia realized that she might have acted somewhat hastily when she had agreed to represent the Letter-Writer. She would definitely be on the A Team Table's dump list if trouble started, and the MAIDS would never speak to her again.

Not that they had ever really spoken more than a few words to her anyway. But still....

The Letter-Writer had hugged Sylvia after she had written the retainer check.

Sylvia put the $5,000 check in her designer handbag and walked briskly out of the bathroom, very pleased with herself after having dispensed her first, valuable legal advice:

"After I leave the bathroom, YOU are NOT, under any circumstances, to leave until after you have counted to 100, the long way—one Mississippi, two Mississippi, and so on. No one must discover that we have been consulting. Talk only to me."

Being a lawyer was all about protecting your client

and in this case, it was critical.

Her client would be forced to leave this school in disgrace, should her identity be discovered.

Doing the math, Sylvia had already earned $500.00 of the retainer. She had conferred with her client in the bathroom, drawn up a Retainer Agreement on the paper towel and given the Letter-Writer instructions not to discuss this complicated case with anyone other than her own attorney.

Sylvia had told her client not to worry about a thing because she had a solid, proven track record as a trial attorney, which was a barefaced lie.

She saw no need to inform the Letter-Writer that her attorney had never filed a real lawsuit of any kind, nor defended one.

Unlike many other law school graduates, she had passed the State Bar Exam the first time she had taken it. Then she had gone back to school to work on a master's degree in philosophy, because law had mostly bored her. She feared that actually practicing it might be unacceptably tedious.

***

*F*our weeks before the Worlds, Sarah arrived at The Table where there was an animated discussion going on about some sort of conspiracy between Irish dance dress designers and adjudicators.

It took several minutes before she had been able to determine exactly what it was that had provoked such like-minded, impassioned outbursts.

Usually, at least a few of the MAIDS disagreed with

a discussion topic, whatever it was, just for the drama it created.

Apparently, it concerned an Irish dance regulation published by the higher powers in Ireland.

None of the MAIDS knew whether or not it was a recently discovered old rule or a new one.

Brandi, shaking her head with shudders of disgust and genuine concern, handed Sarah her phone.

When Sarah had started to laugh as she was reading the Rule, there were gasps of disbelief.

The cold, disapproving, faces of the other MAIDS at The Table, suggested that she might very well be a negligent, deranged mother, if she thought this WIDA Rule, be it a new one or an old, was even remotely funny:

"A dancer may be allowed to re-dance if a Costume malfunction occurs as long as the dancer waits for the adjudicator to ring the bell. If a dancer stops dancing due to a costume malfunction without the adjudicator's permission, the dancer will be disqualified from the competition."

When Sarah was asked why she thought this was so hilarious, she could not answer because she could not breathe from laughing so hard.

She finally managed to suppress her laughter and listened politely to the MAIDS, as they voiced their fears and concerns about the little bell's not ringing.

"What if the adjudicators were texting or working on crossword puzzles, or checking their mail instead of paying close attention?" Valerie asked fearfully.

"How on earth could you ever be certain that one of those adjudicators would ring that little bell?"

"And, will somebody please tell me, just what *is* a costume 'malfunction'?"

After Valerie had left The Table, the MAIDS had decided that most of her 'concern,' was really a catty way of pointing out that none of the other MAIDS' daughters were as well-developed as hers. Therefore, their DDs had much less to worry about concerning a costume's malfunctioning.

The MAIDS had also agreed that this new or old Rule had been printed in too small letters, and that this might have been done deliberately to discourage people from actually reading it. The same way people normally do not read the terms of their appliance purchases, or bank loans, due to the too small print. It was human nature not to read the too small print.

Linda, who had clearly been deep in thought, was about to point out that in this particular instance, not bothering to read the small print might have drastic repercussions.

She stood up and boldly proposed that this so-called 'Bell Ringing Rule' might very well have been drafted after a huge bribe had been offered to Irish dance adjudicators by unknown, ruthless, Irish dance dressmakers.

"What better place on earth could there possibly be to introduce orchestrated costume mayhem than at the Worlds? The place where, unlike at most other Irish dancing events, the odds of a dancer owning a new solo or team dress are actually probable, not just possible."

Linda had the MAIDS' complete attention.

"Their bribe would be for *not* ringing the little bell in a charitable, timely manner, whenever there was a costume malfunction taking place. This would force a dancer to choose between either running off the stage before the bell sounded and being disqualified, or toughing it out, continuing to dance, while waiting for the bell's 'permission to run off the stage' to deal with the malfunction."

Linda took a deep breath and continued rambling on enthusiastically: "This 'Rule' ruse could very well be a ploy by the dressmakers and designers to make truckloads of money by purposely designing dresses with certain sections programmed to fall apart after a predetermined amount of jumping around—just like cars used to begin falling apart, during the golden era of the automotive industry, after a predetermined number of miles."

It was obvious to Linda, as her eyes made contact with each of the MAIDS, that they were not picking up on where she was headed with this complicated plot. She needed to establish some authority.

"I studied this at Vassar," Linda announced.

Again.

She always reminded the other MAIDS, that *she* had gone to Vassar and then to Dartmouth, and that if they had gone to college at all, which many of them had not, they had been awarded their 'easy' degrees by a state university.

"Seriously? You took a class about how to bribe adjudicators at Irish dancing events when you were at Vassar?" Sarah asked.

Linda glanced at Sarah and continued: "As most of you know, I have a degree in Project Engineering Management. I supervise designing, developing and managing new product ideas for corporations."

This was a major revelation to all of the MAIDS, as Linda had never shared with them what her major had been. It sounded as if this Project Engineering major might have given her the proper credentials to pontificate about the Irish dance dressmakers' plot.

"The 'not ringing the bell' threat is most likely a scheme organized by the Irish dressmaking industry to enhance what, as all of us here already know, is their planned 'Obsolescence of Desirability' platform or, if you will, 'Stylistic Obsolescence.' "

The blank looks on the faces of those who were sitting at The Table were unanimous. Sarah had heard about planned obsolescence related to the automotive industry, when car manufacturers in Detroit had, long ago, deliberately designed car parts that needed to be replaced after a certain number of miles, just to keep their profits up. But 'planned obsolescence' in the fashion industry?

Linda continued her controversial lecture.

"As we all know, many products in our society are mostly desirable because of how they look, rather than for practical reasons. Obviously, the best example of this type of product is what we choose to wear."

"None of us here, except of course you, Sarah, can remember hippie attire from the late 1960's and early 70's," Linda said, smiling sweetly, like this was factual.

"Those 'groovy' flower child full-length dresses and bellbottom pants were not around for long, thank goodness! Only the Bohemian and specialty shops sell them now. Unless of course one knows how to shop on Amazon!"

Sarah was furious. What a bitch! How old did this project engineer snoot think she was?

Stifled giggles coming from some of the MAIDS at The Table, reinforced Sarah's intention to get out of this witches' coven right after the Worlds.

Linda was on a fast roll. "Clothing styles have 'hot' periods, which are called fashion cycles."

"By introducing exciting fashions every year or so, using magazines and online seasonal catalogues where last year's looks are gone, and then not producing any of the older designs anymore, clothing manufacturers can pretty much trick the public into buying their new designs, creating a new fashion cycle. The fashionistas keep the money rolling in, cycle after cycle. Mini Skirts are out. Then Mini Skirts are in again. Velvet is great. Then velvet is tacky. You get the idea."

"Sound familiar?" Linda smiled.

64

Sarah was very impressed, in spite of Linda's snide remark about her being considerably older than the other MAIDS. It seemed like Linda knew what she was talking about, and Sarah had to admit that it made sense.

Sarah recalled that once, long ago, her daughter's not-so-old, very much loved solo dress, had been considered 'classic' until, seemingly out of nowhere, it became as desirable as a nun's drab black habit—what Linda had called, "Stylistic Obsolescence."

Later, when Caitlin had outgrown yet another solo dress, Sarah had found that many new dress designs were so 'out there' that they could have been absolute proof for an alternative universe where bad taste was *de rigueur*. She had found a seamstress to let out the seams and extended the outgrown dress's life.

MAID Melissa had become very pale and clammy while she listened to Linda's confusing lecture about cycles of desirability and planned obsolescence.

This awful news might very possibly concern her.

Had she already been unknowingly victimized by all of this? Whatever it was exactly?

Were the three dresses she had ordered for her daughter's first Worlds going to malfunction?

And, if they did not malfunction, were they going to be obsolete by next year's Regional Oireachtas?

If this seemingly paranoid 'conspiracy theory' for Planned Obsolescence was correct, and solo dresses, along with school team dresses, really were going to start malfunctioning on stage at a prescribed time, then it could be too late to do anything about it.

She was already doomed.

Her $14,800 'investment' in Irish dancing *haute couture* and wigs would crash like a devalued currency!

Much, much worse, her beautiful daughter might be totally humiliated on her competition stage when her dresses malfunctioned, and she would be forced to keep on dancing when the bell did not ring so she would not be disqualified.

Melissa seriously considered now, the possibility that perhaps it really had been providential when she ordered the three new expensive solo dresses. Surely, at least *one* of them would hold up at the Worlds?

She raised her hand and when Linda nodded at her, hesitantly asked, "Exactly what do you think is going to happen at the Worlds?"

"Well, I honestly think that this totally ingenious bell-not-ringing scheme is really about creating a vast secondary market," Linda began. "I see a lot of that kind of thing in my profession."

"The malfunctioning parts of the dresses would definitely have to be the sleeves, and not the bodice or the skirt, because who would ever dare take part in compromising the modesty of an Irish dancer?"

"But the sleeves on a dress? Sliding sleeves would certainly interfere with some of the more sensitive dancers' frames of mind, but the stress would not be on a base level, so as to cause total humiliation."

"To eliminate potential stress for dancers, there would need to be identical, interchangeable under-dress-sleeve-protection as an option available to all smart Irish dancing parents. Matching sleeves would have to be made from a lightweight material, and be worn underneath new solo and school dresses in case of an outer dress sleeve malfunction."

"After the Worlds, when word gets out about the sleeves separating and then sliding down the arms of the dancers, there will be an uproar."

"Designers will blame the kinds of material used and certainly the seamstresses would be in the line of fire too. However, the reality would be that no one, except participating conspirators, would really know what had actually happened. How it had been done."

"Under-dress-sleeve-protection will certainly be offered by most of the enterprising designers—in case the malfunction might happen again one day."

"Traditional Irish dance school dresses had so far survived these fashion cycles," Linda had explained, "because they intentionally did not change their basic designs for years at a time—if ever."

Linda thought that this would most probably "no longer be the case," when the Irish dance schools traditional dressmakers discovered the dressmakers' sliding sleeves scheme. They would, of course, want in too."

Linda assured the MAIDS that the dancers were not going to have breakdowns if their sleeves fell off and the designers were certainly not going to involve the younger dancers in their scheme. No one wanted to hear all that hysterical weeping.

She was certain that it would be their daughters' U-13 age category that would be the logical starting point for the 'sliding sleeves scheme.'

"It would be a bonanza for all those dressmakers who had bribed the adjudicators *not* to ring the bell because it would become necessary for consumers' peace of mind to buy expensive, matching sleeves, to be sold along with Irish dance dresses. Comparable to buying car insurance. Meanwhile, guess what? The dressmakers would have already repaired the original sleeves—at no cost."

"A secondary, very lucrative business in the world of Irish dance dress design, would spring forth like Venus from the ocean foam," Linda said.

"So then," Dana responded, "it's like lots, or even most, new dresses have sleeves that will explode or fall apart when they are scheduled to wear out and if your dancer does not have adequate under-dress-sleeve-protection, she'll be exposed to ridicule and humiliation, but keeps on dancing when the bell does *not* ring, so she does not get disqualified."

"Or, she keeps on dancing when the bell does *not* ring but is not going to be totally humiliated because she has matching under-dress-sleeve protection."

Linda smiled appreciatively.

"Precisely."

Linda asked for a show of hands by all MAIDS who had purchased a new solo dress for the Worlds.

The MAIDS who had DDs on the team, but whose daughters were not going to be doing solo steps at the Worlds, sighed with relief, knowing that they had dodged the bullet this time and did not have to worry about a new dress's sleeves exploding!

The other MAIDS who had unfortunately already purchased new solo dresses, did not handle the news well. There were many tears.

Jessica muttered graphic expletives as did Brandi.

Sylvia, due to the fortuitous $5,000 retainer she had received from the Letter-Writer was, while annoyed, not overly concerned.

Since she was now a working lawyer, perhaps she should have cards printed to hand out at the Worlds to parents of the dancers who had lost their sleeves?

A class action lawsuit would have to be prepared quickly before the rest of the legal community heard about it and there was a gold rush.

She would need to print up retainer agreements as well. And take on a large staff of paralegals who might know how to prepare a class action lawsuit.

Undercover detectives, who also knew how to design solo dresses and run sewing machines, would need to be brought on board to gather evidence, and then set up stings to expose the conspirators.

Sylvia also knew that it would be vitally important to name real people or entities in the thousands of lawsuits she and her staff would soon be drafting.

Dana called Therapist Gert immediately and was very happy when Gert promised to meet her at the

Worlds' venue at 7:45 a.m., shortly before her DD's team was scheduled to dance.

Gert would prepare Kaitlin psychologically about how to handle the costume malfunction and how to remain poised when her arms became exposed.

It occurred to Dana that maybe she had better ask Gert to do group therapy with the whole team. Linda had said that all new dresses—both solo and team, were at risk.

***

Sliding sleeves?

Sarah was now convinced that The Top Tier Table MAIDS were seriously unhinged.

Three Weeks Before
The World Irish Dance
Championships

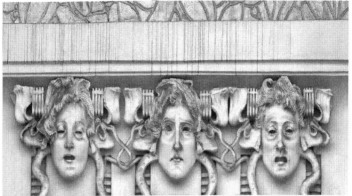

$\mathcal{D}$ance practices had become excruciatingly painful for almost everyone. The MAIDS and The Others had started behaving like the adjudicators did at feiseanna, taking great care not to make direct eye contact with anyone.

The school's dads and all of the male dancers at the intense practices for the Worlds, seemed oblivious to the pressures, and expressed no curiosity as to why all of the MAIDS and some of The Others seemed to be coming unglued around them.

Most of the men took evasive action, keeping their distance, pretending to be immersed in reading thick books or newspapers.

The dance instructors at the school walked around looking like haggard martyrs.

Everyone knew that Sylvia knew who had written that offensive letter, but Sylvia was not going to reveal, or even hint, at the identity of her client. It had been strictly applied, 'attorney-client confidentiality' inside the dance school's restroom on the day the confession had taken place.

The dance school's staff was very annoyed that the guilty mother had confessed to the only lawyer-mom among the ranks of the school mothers.

How cunning was that?

The T.C.R.G. and her assistants now feared that they might never find out who had written that letter.

Anxiety about the bell's failure to ring after there had been a dress-sleeve incident, ran rampant when the word got out, and went around the school many times. No one wanted their daughter to be the first casualty.

Some of The Others had called their dressmakers to express genuine concern and considerable outrage but their complaints fell upon deaf ears.

Neither designers nor dressmakers would own up and admit that there was soon going to be a need for matching under-dress-sleeve-protection.

**

*B*randi had never, not in her wildest dreams, dared to imagine that she would have the opportunity to start a major pre-Worlds Voy Forum war. Yet now, here she was, planning to launch her attack in just one more week—two weeks before the Worlds, that would make Worlds history.

She had begun her strategic maneuvers by visiting the most offensive chat forums every day and writing down the most insulting comments she could find.

Brandi had employed many of these same vitriolic insults herself over the years, but now she wanted to construct, for her own use, an Irish Dance Voy Forum Dictionary-Thesaurus. She wanted to bolster up her 'unnerving' vocabulary arsenal of insults, and to list taunts that she had already used, so she could recycle them. Most of her time was spent in compiling words and phrases such as:

goon/pathetic/clod/disgusting/twit/lame/
dolt/dork/repulsive/whiny/simpleton/boor/
ignorant/uninformed/half-
wit/shallow/donkey/
obtuse/gross/crude/vulgar/dense/ churlish/
You are so obviously trolling
Your school is probably poaching dancers
Your Personality Disorder has no place here
Stop vomiting all over everyone! Loser!
Wow! Just Wow! Moron!
Snarky loser
Let it go lame brain
Bitch slap down time
Love how you are too scared to use your name
Stop fixating airhead
Get off your pathetic high horse
If you had just acted in a timely manner
How offensive can someone be, maniac!

Many post here under the guise of a TC
Mea Culpa, Mea Culpa, idiot
Are you the one who is always pointing out the
"less talented dancers?"
Put the blame where it belongs sister
You certainly get around all the boards, don't you?
Internet troll
Karma to you
Bait for school gossip
What a paranoid, always thinking the posts are
about you, aren't you?
A bunch of sorry-assed losers

She thought she knew who the mothers were at her
own school who dabbled regularly on the Irish Dance
Voy Forums, pretending that they were only voyeurs,
not regular Voyers.

Brandi never let on that she suspected them. It was
not difficult to figure out their identity. Eventually, a
Voyer would drop an unintentional hint, like a driller's
name, which would directly point to the dance school
they were associated with.

Brandi had always thought of the busy chatrooms
as frontiers of opportunity to play intimidation games.

Her pre-Worlds debut on the forums, would begin
by describing the painful, anonymous letter that had
been delivered by the USPS to her T.C.R.G. There had
been no return address.

Then she would fling lightning bolts of accusations
at the most hostile, and thus most susceptible, targets

she had identified.

She would accuse each of them of having written that vicious letter to her daughter's unnamed T.C.R.G. for the sole purpose of undermining school morale before the Worlds: "What kind of 'monster' would do such a thing?" And so on....

The veteran Voyers would become puffed up with pettiness and denial until the final days leading up to the World Championships. And if she did it right, even during the Worlds itself.

If the Letter-Writer did not become known before the Worlds, Brandi could expect the Worlds, on some levels anyway, to turn into a major fiasco at her own school, with suspicious MAIDS and The Others, eying their suspects until the first day of competitions and ignoring their daughters' own needs at a stressful time.

They would have an excuse to drink too much and then easily lose their tempers and reveal far too much about how they really felt about their DDs' teachers and some of the MAIDS and The Others as well.

Sometimes Brandi felt almost giddy planning to inflict punishment upon this hypocritical community which had caused her daughter to cry herself to sleep so many nights, one disappointment after another.

She feared that the real Letter-Writer might surface before the Worlds. If that happened, it might ruin everything. Brandi wished that *she* had written the letter that had created so much chaos.

As things were, the opportunity to wreak havoc on one's adversaries at the World Championships might, like some comets, come only once in a lifetime.

She would use sinister phrases on Voy such as: "I know who you are, bitch" and "I know exactly what you have done. You think you have been so clever, but I'm on to you. Better be careful, you clueless THOT, I'm watching you…"

'THOT' was an unfamiliar word to Brandi. She had had to look it up in the Urban Dictionary to find out how insulting and disgusting it was.

***

*M*ichelle easily found the address of an Urgent Care Clinic which was located only fifteen miles from her regular doctor's office. Katelyn was in a great deal of pain, having unknowingly stopped taking Tylenol after the two tablets her mother had given her had worn off.

Michelle had dumped the rest of the Tylenol and replaced it with Nectasweet artificial sweetener tablets.

She had done this, not only because Tylenol was harmful for her daughter's fragile stomach, but also because, if she were going to get another cortisone shot, Katelyn needed to be convincingly hurting when they walked into the new clinic. She was a dancer— not an actress. She might only be given a knee brace, denied a cortisone injection and referred back to her primary physician, if Michelle were to depend on her daughter's acting ability to receive immediate care.

There were only three weeks left until the Worlds. Katelyn *had* to have the pain relief right now, if she were going to be able to practice. Then, just one more shot to get through the World Championships.

When Katelyn was sobbing, and no longer able to endure the terrible pain, Michelle drove to the clinic. She parked at the main entrance and ran inside to find a wheelchair.

She pushed Katelyn through the revolving doors, into the large reception area, and asked to see a doctor immediately. Her daughter, obviously in a great deal of pain, waited patiently as large tears streamed down her contorted face.

Michelle easily got the much needed cortisone shot that Doctor Horan had so rudely refused to administer to Katelyn, along with a promise that there could be up to three more injections at the new clinic.

The Urgent Care doctor's daughter happened to be an Irish dancer too. She fully understood how painful knee problems could be.

Her own daughter was wearing a boot and would not be able to dance again for some time.

She explained that after the next shot, there would have to be an MRI before she would be able to justify a third one.

Michelle assured the doctor-dance-mom, that one more shot after this one would be fine. Today's shot would get her daughter through practices.

The next shot would get her through the Worlds.

The Urgent Care doctor told Michelle to "hang in there," and wished her new patient the "luck of the Irish." Michelle sighed with gratitude.

Finally, there was plenty of pain-free time to get through the dance practices and a final injection would be available for the Worlds.

Having outsmarted smug Doctor Horan, Michelle acknowledged, had given her great pleasure.

***

Sylvia often reflected during the three weeks leading up to the Worlds about whether or not her daughter, Sub #1, was going to get the chance to dance on the U-13 8-Hand Céilí A Team.

It was unrealistic to hope that there might actually be a sick or injured A Team dancer who would be out of commission.

Still, it was very pleasant daydreaming about such a possibility.

She went over the prospects.

Realistically, there were four DDs on the team who looked very 'iffy' to Sylvia.

One was far too thin and her fair complexion had turned sallow. Sylvia suspected that her loving mother, Stacey, was under-feeding her DD or encouraging her to throw up. Probably Stacey was helping her vomit. There was little doubt in Sylvia's mind, that Stacey's fragile daughter was either bulimic or anorexic, with her mother's approval.

Sylvia could easily see that Michelle's daughter was trying to mask severe knee pain. Sylvia wondered how many cortisone shots it would take to get her on the stage.

Valerie's daughter was still dealing with the terrible sunburn she had brought back with her from her trip to Mexico. Her skin was peeling and she was covered with lotions. She could barely lift her arms.

The painful sunburn, however, was showing signs of improvement and would probably heal completely over the next few weeks, unless there would be some blistering complications. Not likely, but perhaps not entirely wishful thinking.

There *could* be blisters.

By far the most likely not-to-make-it dancer, was Jessica's ashen-faced daughter who had suffered a bad seizure recently during practice.

That looked very hopeful, but knowing Jessica, her unfortunate DD would have to be almost dead before her mother would permit her to yield her rightful place on the team to a Sub.

After that recent seizure, Jessica had said, "Well, I think it's time for a short break."

Not time for the ER? Time for a *short break*?

Sylvia seriously doubted Jessica's sanity.

At least my Caytlin has her solo steps to look forward to at the World Championships, Sylvia consoled herself.

***

*S*ylvia was really much more concerned about what to do with the timid Letter-Writer, thinking again that perhaps she should not have been so hasty to draw up that binding Retainer Agreement in the bathroom on the Bounty paper towel.

As things stood now, she was standing by, on the job, waiting to see what was going to happen. So far, things had gotten somewhat uglier, but mothers had refrained from removing their DDs from the school, despite believing, 'where there's smoke, there's fire.'

She had found her old law school torts class notes and scheduled an appointment with the Letter-Writer at a twenty-four hour McDonald's, in a city fifty miles away from the dance school, to make sure that it was far enough away to provide complete privacy.

It was also possible that Sylvia's house was being watched. She could only hope that she was not going to be followed when she left to meet the Letter-Writer.

The meeting took place at 4:00 a.m.

Both parties shook hands, sat down and pulled out the safety tabs in their large McDonald's coffees.

Sylvia began her lawyer-client consultation, hoping she could keep it going until she had earned at least a thousand dollars. She would have to talk slower and pause a lot for dramatic effect.

"If our school were to close, because of something you had *said*, that could consist of damages against you if a lawsuit was brought. But it is not enough to *prove* that what you wrote in your letter somehow led to the damages," Sylvia paused briefly, then plowed on.

"We all have both freedom of speech and freedom of press in this country. Freedom of press applies not only to the printed word, but to letters as well."

"If it can be proven that you wrote the letter, then it would fall under the law of 'libel,' one of the two kinds of defamation. The other kind of defamation is called 'slander,' the spoken word."

"However, they must prove that, not only you *wrote* the letter, but also that *what you wrote was defamatory.*

That is, that it subjected her—or your school—to hatred, ridicule, or contempt"

Sylvia looked up from her notes before she went on, just as the Letter-Writer's head fell forward and banged on the table.

Before Sylvia could process how alarming this was, the Letter-Writer perked up and apologized profusely for falling asleep.

"This is not as bad as you think," Sylvia comforted, "because the letter you have shown me is clearly *not* defamatory, even though other people's interpretation may be."

"But what *they* might say is irrelevant and certainly not caused by you. Plus, the truth of what is written is an absolute defense if it can be proven to be true."

Sylvia was elated that she was sounding like a real lawyer. So far, things had been going just how she had hoped.

By explaining defamation facts in great detail to her distraught client, she was both commanding respect from the Letter-Writer, as well as gaining much needed self-confidence, by pretending to be talking to a jury. She was also running up her fee.

Sylvia could clearly hear the iconic Chariots of Fire movie soundtrack starting as she continued:

"And even if the letter is proven to be written by you and to be defamatory, we *still* win because you did not publish it!"

"The final necessity for the maintenance of a claim for defamation is that you make it public, to at least one third party, and you did not."

"*They* did!"

"You sent the letter to the person claiming to have been defamed."

"*SHE HERSELF* chose to share it—publish it—with others."

"So if she—or the school—was defamed, it was *her* fault not yours!"

She put a closing argument spin on her summation to the jury speech: "Ultimately, it all comes down to what the judge or the jury, believes to be true."

"I repeat, what my client has written, that so many misguided others have greatly misrepresented, might be actionable against *them* but not my client."

"Ladies and Gentlemen of the Jury, you must find my client, NOT GUILTY—in the eyes of Almighty God and this great State."

Pausing again for impact, she turned her gaze back to the seat opposite hers and was surprised to see that the Letter-Writer was no longer sitting in it.

She looked under the table and was relieved to observe that her client did not seem to be down there.

She craned her neck and looked behind her before she remembered that they had been seated at the very back of the McDonald's and there was only a wall.

As a last resort, she stood up and looked straight ahead, in the direction of the fast food pickup counter. Maybe her client had become hungry and had quietly slipped away while she was practicing how to impress a jury?

A crowd had gathered and was blocking her view of the counter. Sylvia sauntered towards the group.

Upon further investigation, she saw that her client had passed out on the floor in front of the Ladies' Room.

EMTs were racing through the front door.

She wondered how long her client had been down on the floor before she had discovered that the Letter-Writer had left their table.

The impulse to rush to her client was tempered by a lawyer's caution to 'get all the facts first.'

As she readied herself to act as a lawyer on behalf of a client for the first time, she carefully surveyed the landscape for possible pitfalls.

Seeing nothing obvious, to psych herself up for her formal debut, she quietly whispered excerpts from the oath she had made and memorized the day she had been inducted by the State Bar:

"I, do solemnly swear that I will support the Constitution of the United States and the Constitution of this State.

I will maintain the respect due to courts of justice and judicial officers; I will not counsel or maintain any suit or proceeding that shall appear to me to be without merit or to be unjust; I will not assert any defense except such as I honestly believe to be debatable under the law of the land;

I will maintain the confidence and preserve inviolate the secrets of my client...

I will at all times faithfully and diligently adhere to the rules of professional responsibility and a lawyer's creed of professionalism of the State Bar. AMEN"

Her shrewd legal instincts were instantly rewarded when she saw that one of the EMTs was one of **The Others**!

In spite of all of the elaborate, seemingly needless precautions, the impossible had happened.

Sylvia pivoted.

Without so much as a hesitation, or a parting glance in the direction of the emergency unfolding on the floor in front of the Ladies' Restroom, she walked out the back door.

She wondered which of the cars parked in the back lot belonged to The Letter-Writer.

A lawyer's job was to protect her client.

Two Weeks Before
The World Irish Dance
Championships

Lasciate ogne speranza, voi ch'intrate

$\mathcal{D}$ante's Divine Comedy describes nine circles of hell. However, there was a tenth circle that he did not know about: **The Second Week Before The World Irish Dance Championships.**

Linda had taken note of the whispering among The Others in the halls, when she and her DD had arrived for classes, exactly two weeks and two days before the Worlds.

She did not recall having seen any of these Others before, but they nodded at her as she passed by them on her way to The Table.

She returned their nods with the kind of resigned smile reserved for distant in-laws at holiday gatherings. She wondered why she had never noticed them lurking about before.

They were certainly chattering energetically about something. Whatever it was, it could not be of interest to her.

When Linda reached The Table, she was greeted by an obviously alarmed Stacey: "Thank goodness you're here. Have you heard the news?"

"What news?" Linda replied.

"We will need to find a replacement T.C.R.G. to get us through the Worlds because ours is at home staring at the walls and not speaking," Michelle said frantically.

"You mean she's catatonic?" Linda was beginning to worry. The A Team still needed some fine tuning and the DDs might be devastated and lose some of their punch.

"What happened?" Linda finally managed to ask.

"No one is sure," Valerie said flatly, wondering if her DD's second degree sunburn was still going to be problematic in two weeks. It was much better, but her daughter still had difficulty lifting her arms. Neither of them had spoken to each other for weeks. Valerie was not sure she would ever be able to bring herself to talk to her disobedient daughter again. And if she ever met up again with Ann—God help that little bitch.

"Well this is just great," Linda snapped. "And just *what* are all of us supposed to do if her replacement is an incompetent ass, buy some lucky charms and cross our fingers?"

"It happened because of all those dreadful rumors going around," Melissa said softly. "That sent her right over the edge. She went right off the cliff when she found out everybody in this school knew all about the letter and had started telling lies and making up stories about her private life," Melissa said, choking back a sob.

"There was nothing sensational in that letter we all read!" Linda proclaimed impatiently.

The T.C.R.G. had only chosen the trusted, tenured MAIDS to share the anonymous letter with, and it was slowly dawning on everyone that one or more of them at The Table had apparently 'talked.'

The T.C.R.G. had requested them to keep their ears open as to any rumors they might hear with regard to the horrid letter and she had demanded their complete discretion before she had permitted them to read it.

Several of the First Tier tenured MAIDS had told a few of their old, 'trusted' friends, who were still part of The Others, about the letter. But they knew better than to ever admit they had done that.

The Others had been flattered to be included in a

Top Tier Table issue. The MAIDS who had squealed, had trusted The Others they had confided in, to keep their eyes and ears open and their mouths shut, and to report back to them if they discovered any pertinent facts.

"Well, it sounds like there have been several pretty outrageous rumors going around about her for the last few weeks," Stacey put in.

"The poor thing only found out when five mothers approached her last night and informed her that they were considering removing their daughters from our school because she was such an unfit person," Stacey revealed, wearing an anguished expression on her face.

"Unfit?" Jessica questioned, from the far end of The Table.

"You know, like she was an overall 'unfit' person," a disembodied voice at The Table added.

Jessica was amazed and somewhat confounded.

"How much fitter can anyone be?" she demanded. "I see her at Curves almost every time I go there."

"We are not talking about her physical condition, moron," Stacey replied, exasperated.

"What *are* you talking about, then, slut?" Jessica shrieked back.

"I am *talking* about her *moral fitness*," Stacey snarled, lowering her heavy Southern drawl to a growl.

"What morale fitness?" Jessica was now thoroughly confused. "Her morale has always been inspirational!" Jessica insisted.

Before Stacey had the chance to deliver a knockout

punch to Jessica's obviously limited ability to fence with words delivered by someone who spoke with a heavy Southern accent, Michelle cut in, "Come on! That is quite enough, bimbos. We need to be strong for our daughters now. There is no room for bickering. And there's no turning back."

***

*T*he anonymous letter had taken on a life of its own. Mary, an Other mother from one of the U-10 teams, said that someone, whose name she would not reveal, had texted her that their T.C.R.G. was having a torrid affair with one of the husbands of an unnamed school mom and that the wife-dance-mom was clueless.

The widespread texting gossip included the 'fact' that their T.C.R.G. had received an anonymous letter accusing her of being an adulteress.

This rumor had made many of The Others on the second and third tiers look at their bubbly T.C.R.G. in a completely different way, questioning now why she always seemed to be so happy.

Another version of the secret letter was described by Pamela, a nosy, whiny Other that most people tried to avoid on the second tier. Pamela said that she had heard that their T.C.R.G. suspected that the letter had been written by her BFF from grade school because the Letter-Writer had very specifically mentioned Saint Macrina the Younger Grade School.

How could she do this to her oldest best friend? It was disgusting.

One of The Others had excitedly confirmed that

was indeed where their T.C.R.G. had gone to school from sixth through eighth grade. She knew this for a fact thanks to her youngest brother having had a major crush on her back then.

The worst rumor circulating throughout the entire school in hushed tones, was that their T.C.R.G. had received a certified letter from the District Attorney's Office. The letter had notified her of an Initial Court Appearance date and Pretrial Conference, for either her fourth, as some of The Others maintained, or her fifth DUI offense, as others of The Others insisted.

Whether fourth or fifth, the letter had generously offered a Plea Agreement deal of five years with work-release privileges.

So their T.C.R.G. would be permitted to supervise and teach dance classes at the school seven days a week and then return late each night to sleep in the Work Release Dorm with all the other women prisoners.

Naturally, she would have to take a breathalyzer test every time she checked back in for the night.

Also, she would not be permitted by the Court to travel out of state to an Oireachtas or Worlds, until her DUI sentence had been completed, because of all the booze that would be available at those events.

***

After Jessica had managed to calm down considerably from her word-fencing with Stacey, she looked around suspiciously and accused all the MAIDS at The Table of having betrayed their T.C.R.G.'s trust by "flapping their yaps."

Sarah was still not sitting at The Table, and Jessica considered whether this might be of any significance. Was Sarah *hiding* from the MAIDS?

Like a reptile ready to strike and swallow its prey, Jessica focused her beady black eyes on the MAIDS, one by one, moving from left to right.

Melissa had a brief impression of snakes slithering around all over Jessica's head when Jessica's eyes were fixed on her.

It is totally time to stop drinking, she thought, as the dark eyes finished probing her brain and moved away like a spotlight on a moonless night, heading towards Brandi.

Melissa felt like she had been turned to stone.

When all of the MAIDS still present at the A Team Table, had finished denying having ever discussed the anonymous letter with anyone outside of their Table group of friends, Jessica hissed:

"Liars!"

What happened next almost caused the MAIDS to laugh, but they did not, in view of the fact that it was so horrifying.

Jessica removed a folded up brown paper lunch bag from her purse and without comment, placed the bag over her mouth and hawk-like nose.

Her penetrating eyes continued to move from face to face at The Table, while she breathed in the bag. She looked like an anteater.

When she had finally finished breathing in the bag, she asked, "Sylvia dear, can you please recommend a good attorney to file a libel lawsuit on behalf of this school against your Letter-Writing client? But perhaps I should handle this lawsuit myself?"

Melissa would afterwards swear that Jessica's eyes had rolled up backwards in her head and that her tiny tongue had been forked when she stuck it in and out of her mouth at Sylvia, like a three-year-old child.

Jessica was really a lawyer? She hadn't known the difference between 'moral' and 'morale' so it might be possible, thought Brandi, writing herself a note in the pad she always kept on hand now to record possible attack words for her Voy Insults Dictionary-Thesaurus.

She knew how much her ex-husband had detested lawyer jokes. He took them personally because he was probably guilt-ridden over his shortcomings when he had practiced law before becoming disbarred.

The rest of the MAIDS, except for Jessica, who had begun breathing into another paper lunch bag and Sarah, who was still missing, were busy decompressing themselves, taking great care not to look each other in the eye in case they might project a guilty conscience.

***

Dana was far too busy worrying about why there had been no sign of her daughter, Kaitlin, having started a growth spurt, to become preoccupied with the identity of the Letter-Writer.

It had been a few weeks of injections and there was nothing to show for it. She sometimes wondered why she had even bothered.

Her husband had exploded with anger when, after

complaining about his having to pick up their four-year-old, pigtailed twins at daycare, and then prepare dinner, she had explained to him why Kaitlin and she were gone on Tuesdays and Thursdays.

There were the hormone shots at the growth clinic and then off to dance.

He had acted like she was insane and perhaps even dangerous and so on....

Blah, blah, blah.

Even worse, much worse, her daughter was being a terribly bad sport about growing, insisting she did not *care* if she were taller, which of course was not true.

She screamed like a two month old baby getting its first shots every time a needle came near her.

It was very nerve-wracking.

When Dana interrogated the six endocrinologists on her DD's medical team about why her daughter was not yet a little bit taller, they dismissed her concerns with, "What did you expect, Dana? Magic beans? This is not Jack and the Beanstalk. This will take time. Lots of time. Surely you did not expect to see results in the first several weeks?"

Their condescending tone made it obvious that, if she did admit that she *had* hoped for signs of growth, they would think she was somewhat dimwitted. So she had remained silent.

Those bullies had no idea what it was like, hoping and sometimes praying, that your too-short daughter was going to sprout up like an early spring crocus.

Jack and the Beanstalk was her favorite fairy tale.

And, if the truth be told, she *had* found the goose that laid the golden eggs when she had married a rich man.

So why *not* those magic beans now?

***

Stacey was worried that she might have gone a bit too far with her motherly attempts at helping her daughter to control her fluctuating weight.

Caitlyn's complexion was beginning to resemble an aging banana and the palms of her hands were turning orange.

There were fewer than fourteen days left until the Worlds. Stacey decided that she might have to back off Caitlyn for a bit—let her eat and not encourage her to empty the contents of her stomach afterwards.

She certainly did not want her DD to look like one of those odd little Oompa Loompas in Willie Wonka's chocolate factory.

Her DD's complexion would noticeably clash with her lime green solo dress and there was neither money nor time to get a new one.

When Stacey remembered that the team had made reservations for team tanning the night before they danced, she relaxed.

Surely the tanning spray would mask her daughter's sallow skin tones?

***

Linda had decided that yoga exercise and relaxation techniques would replace soccer for now, and be even better for her daughter than aerobics.

Besides, Kaetlin already jumped around more than

enough doing her Irish dancing steps.

She needed to be deep breathing now, visualizing that gold medal. Holding it in her hands.

Preparing for transformation was vitally important before a major life event.

***

*L*inda knew this firsthand, because she had been on her college tennis team and in her senior year, her team had made it to the final rounds in her conference.

After team practices, she had applied visualization techniques and spent most of her unscheduled time, visualizing tennis balls being lobbed back and forth by an unmanned racquet.

Even though the constant tennis ball lobbing made her dizzy, she kept at it.

Once, when one of her professors had asked her to remain after class for a short discussion, she had been thrilled. She thought she had made some interesting observations during the art history lecture that day.

However, the teacher did not want to discuss her insights. Rather, Ms. Frost had asked if she was going through a "difficult time" lately—that her eyes were moving back and forth like she was following a ping pong ball and was she perhaps depressed?

***

*Y*oga would connect her daughter to the universal power that pervades everything.

After the Worlds, she would have to make a list of visual images for Kaetlin to use for her yoga classes.

The tennis balls had worked well for herself, but since her daughter did not yet play tennis—her list of inspiring visual images would have to wait until after it was determined whether her swim team would win the State championship and then be going on to the Nationals.

In the meantime, it was very important that Kaetlin experienced self-realization and inner peace.

The kind of self-actualization that she, her mother, had achieved over the years in her spare time.

One Week Before
The World Irish Dance
Championships
The Bonding Party

*N*one of the MAIDS were looking forward to the mandatory team bonding party that Jessica would be hosting one week before the Worlds. Her daughter, Catelyn, sickly as she was, had been elected team captain. Or so Jessica had *said* after she had counted the paper ballots herself.

Jessica's daughter having been duly elected was fine with all the other MAIDS, who knew that hosting the obligatory bonding party was the duty of the céilí team captain, which meant that the food preparation and activities were passed on to the team captain's primary caregiver.

When the compliant MAIDS and their reluctant DDs arrived at Jessica's tidy looking, redbrick house, they were astonished to find that Jessica had not only removed all the furniture in the living room, she had also roped off the stairs leading up to the second floor.

The MAIDS were more than a little bit put off by this. What did Jessica think they were going to do? Lift her bath towels? Steal her toothbrush?

There were six fold up chairs set up, lining one of the living room walls. Only a table remained in Jessica's small kitchen; the four table chairs had been relocated to the living room and placed along the wall opposite the fold up chairs. All of the chairs on both sides of the room were placed on mats so as not to scratch the beautiful red pine floor.

No one knew quite what to do or where to go. Six DDs sat on the uncomfortable fold up chairs. The rest of them sat on the floor, cross-legged. All of the DDs had quickly escaped into their phones to relieve the awkwardness that everyone felt.

The MAIDS stayed in the small kitchen, standing, and the unoccupied kitchen chairs in the living room, remained unoccupied.

Jessica announced that their team captain, Catelyn, had a terrible headache and pointed her out sleeping in a corner of the living room in a pink sleeping bag.

The MAIDS in the tiny kitchen felt like they were standing at a bus stop without a bench.

There was no food in sight, only the desserts that each of the guest MAIDS had contributed.

Jessica wandered around, handing out three ounce Dixie paper cups.

Sarah watched peculiar Jessica making her rounds and thought the un-healthy looking A Team members looked even more fragile here, away from the familiar dance school environment.

Jessica's daughter was by far the worst. She looked dreadful. Her face was white as a sheet peeking out from her sleeping bag. Sarah had become increasingly alarmed at the lack of expression in Catelyn's eyes and the way she seemed to always be dizzy, crashing into things—except that there were no 'things' to crash into at dance practices. Mostly, she crashed into other people—like she had no sense of space or direction anymore. That girl needed an MRI to rule out a brain tumor. What was *wrong* with Jessica?

One of the MAIDS was going to have to get her nerve up and tell Jessica that her daughter was not well enough to continue on to the World Championships. The T.C.R.G. should logically be the one to inform Jessica that Sub #1 was going to have to step in, but Sarah suspected the TC had lost her confidence after the anonymous letter fiasco, which was still unsolved, thanks to Sylvia.

There was also the reality that everyone knew that telling Jessica her daughter was "out," would be on the level of an international nuclear missile crisis. None of the MAIDS could imagine how angrily Jessica would react and they were not going to voluntarily find out.

Stacey's daughter looked gaunt and jaundiced. Not

nearly so sick as Jessica's daughter, but she too needed an immediate medical evaluation.

Just when the tension had become palpable, a pizza delivery truck appeared in the driveway. Jessica must have assumed that she had told everyone about the pizza menu. There were groans of thankfulness from the DDs, who were starving.

A delivery man approached the door carrying two medium to large size pizzas. Jessica paid the man and ceremoniously announced with what seemed like great pride that, "there would be 'a' piece for everyone."

Since 'everyone' was ten mothers and ten hungry young ladies, the more generous mothers deferred to their daughters, claiming they were not hungry so their own daughter could have two pieces.

Stacey took a slice for herself and then handed her daughter the smallest one she could find. The World Championships were only two weeks away and she would be damned if her careless daughter was going to gorge on two pieces of pizza. One was bad enough.

Sylvia noticed Stacey depriving her skinny daughter of food which was no surprise.

Valerie, also calorie conscious, beat her DD to the pizza box and removed a small segment for her little sunburned idiot, handing it over wordlessly.

Jessica walked around with a large pitcher of water and insisted that each of the dancers have at least two cups so they would not risk dehydration. She watched each of them as they drank the three ounces, moving out only after she had poured the second three ounces.

Jessica returned from the living room to pour water for the MAIDS gathered around the kitchen table.

Other than the water squirting from Sarah's nose as she tried unsuccessfully to suppress her laughter while drinking, there was little merriment to be found at the bonding party. The guests began to plot their retreats.

Sylvia had already left with her daughter. She had seemed distant throughout the gathering. There was something obviously on her mind which the MAIDS attributed to her representing the Letter-Writer. The stress level at the school had gone from bad to boiling point. If Sylvia was stressed out, she had no one to blame but herself.

The hungriest team dancers had moved back into the kitchen to devour the desserts on the table next to the empty pizza boxes. Some MAIDS thanked Jessica for a lovely party and then gave their daughters a 'let's get out of here now' look. Most simply fled.

Jessica seemed unconcerned that the party guests were leaving, fixating instead on the 'piggy' dancers who were still at the trough, stuffing their mouths with fattening desserts. She observed with disgust that most of them were laughing with their mouths open, *the little porkers....*

The MAIDS had not honored her request to bring only healthy desserts. She would have never ordered the pizza had she known the MAIDS were going to be so irresponsible. Oatmeal raisin cookies and banana bread were not fit for human consumption.

The 'piggy' DDs, who were not as polite as their

mothers, had escaped through the back door after they had seen how Jessica was looking at them—like she would turn them to stone if she could. Some of them stuffed a few cookies into their training bras as they offered their thanks and ran for their lives.

The team bonding party had lasted approximately twenty-five minutes, including the wait for the pizza delivery truck. There were no inexpensive, sentimental gifts, hardly any food or conversation and nothing to do but get out as soon as possible.

Sarah, who was the last MAID to escape, thanked Jessica and let herself out the front door. As she made her way towards the porch steps, she heard a vacuum cleaner start up in the living room.

She had almost reached the stairs, when her right peripheral vision glimpsed colorful pots on the other side of the porch. She moved closer, to get a better look at them on the concrete floor, hidden behind a plastic chair.

She could see that there were tiny flowering plants peeking out of the pots. The temperature a few days ago had dropped down to twenty-nine cold degrees. Hardly weather conducive to the survival of plants on an unenclosed porch.

Since Jessica seemed like such an anal control freak, Sarah was surprised that she would subject her plants to such harsh outside conditions.

Even the warmest days were only in the low forties. Sarah decided to have a look at the hardy specimens.

She was tired of often losing her own early-planted

outdoor flowers to unexpected frosts.

She was thinking that maybe she could ask Jessica how she had managed to keep them alive out here on this open porch, exposing them to the cold air seeping in through the wrought iron railings, when disturbing thoughts entered her head.

These pots must have been inside until the party. The weather has been far too cold for them to thrive out here on the porch like this. They are even flowering! Why had they been moved outside on the porch almost out of sight? Why not put them on the kitchen counters if Jessica wanted to make sure no one broke the pots? Or a windowsill...

She had the alarming explanation after she moved in close enough to see what was growing in the pots. Sarah realized she was a pharmacist, not a botanist, but she was absolutely positive that she saw foxglove, one of the most toxic flowering plants anywhere on earth. 'Dead Men's Bells' was her favorite descriptive phrase for foxglove. It was a beautiful plant but not worth the risk of cultivating.

Sarah's mind raced, recalling the many people over the years who had come to her pharmacy covered with hives to ask what to do after just *touching* foxglove. In the right doses, ingesting foxglove was usually 100% fatal. Anyone who had been unfortunate enough to have done that, did not seek her advice—they had died quickly from cardiac arrest.

It was time to get out before the vacuum cleaner switched off and Jessica discovered her looking at the foxglove plants, which she had obviously taken great care to place out of view.

Sarah hurriedly took two pictures with her phone, holding it down low at her side, away from the window she had noticed directly to her left. She fled down the porch steps, very happy that behind her, the humming vacuum cleaner continued searching for crumbs.

Why would anyone grow foxglove on their porch? Perhaps Jessica was really that dumb? But was it only a coincidence that Sarah had suspected for some time that Jessica's daughter was exhibiting almost textbook symptoms of acute cyanide poisoning?

Had Jessica been giving her daughter cyanide? Was she going to switch to foxglove?

It felt like she had just walked into one of Agatha Christie's murder by poison mysteries. Except that so far, there had not been a victim—at least one that she was aware of.

Sarah knew that foxglove could cause cardiac arrest which mimicked a normal heart attack. If an autopsy was not performed, which was often the case if the circumstances surrounding a death did not appear to be suspicious, the murderer got away with it.

Sarah asked herself the same questions over and over: was it just a coincidence that Jessica's daughter's health had started to crash five weeks ago and there were poisonous plants growing on Jessica's tidy porch? Until recently, her daughter had always seemed like a normal person. Too quiet perhaps, definitely closed-mouth, but not on a mother's radar screen for being a possible victim of poisoning.

She was certain that Jessica's daughter was showing classic signs of cyanide poisoning—the slow way. Not in amounts that would kill her quickly, but over a period of time.

The kitchen at Jessica's had been mostly stripped bare but the kitchen's counters had not.

Sarah had seen a large Mason Jar without a lid, that was next to what looked like vintage Franciscan Ware canisters. She had been surprised that fussy Jessica had allowed a plain jar to share space with the attractive *Coffee*, *Flour* and *Sugar* stoneware. She remembered that the glass jar was filled with what looked like large, dry beans. She thought they were lima beans because they were pale green.

She had been surprised in pharmacy school when she had learned that lima beans contained cyanide and if eaten raw, could be lethal. She knew that in the U.S., there were restrictions in place about cyanide levels in commercially grown lima beans, but who knew where Jessica might have purchased hers?

If she were deliberately giving her delicate daughter raw and/or undercooked lima beans, she could very possibly be poisoning her with cyanide to set up the 'scenario' for a sudden death from foxglove—digitalis.

Jessica often brought little brown paper treat bags to class for her daughter which supposedly contained 'power nuts' to keep Catelyn's stamina up. Until now, Sarah had not thought that had been suspicious. She knew that high levels of cyanide prevent oxygen from getting into the blood and can eventually cause death.

Jessica was doing it slowly. No wonder her daughter had looked cyanotic-gray at times.

Sarah spent Saturday night confirming her worst fears about Jessica's foxglove and reviewing cyanide lima bean poisoning in her old textbooks and online.

As preposterous as the thought seemed, she now feared that Jessica was poisoning her own daughter.

The Southwest Neurological Clinic where Jessica had told the MAIDS she had been taking her daughter, had probably not tested Catelyn for traces of cyanide. That would never have happened unless Jessica had carelessly revealed her true mentally ill self, which was unlikely.

Sarah tried to stop the crazy melodrama now being enacted in her head: *the foxglove-digitalis would be Jessica's grand finale poison. Her daughter was already drastically weakened by the cyanide 'snacks' and the digitalis found in the leaves and stems of the foxglove plants would cause a quick, massive, fatal heart attack.*

Why would anyone suspect Jessica? Sarah knew Jessica was a shrew straight out of hell, but she could easily masquerade as a caring mother when she had to. Sarah had seen her do it. The last thing a doctor would suspect was that it was the 'concerned mother' who was making her daughter deathly ill.

Sarah remembered Catelyn had never displayed any acutely ill health symptoms until the past few weeks—after the U-13 team had been chosen. So it had been going on for weeks, not months, ever since the team practices for the Worlds had begun.

Even though it was obvious to anyone who knew Jessica, that her daughter seemed to be her *raison d'etre*, Sarah had an almost overwhelming sense of dread that Jessica was every bit as crazy as she seemed to be—but with an evil twist.

Sarah's intuition told her that Jessica was going to administer a lethal dose of foxglove to her daughter at the Worlds—probably right before the céilí team went on stage so her daughter would collapse seconds after the team dance had begun.

How could this be happening in the presence of so many mothers? The irony was painful. Especially since one of them was a pharmacist—someone who had already seen the horror of Munchausen Syndrome by Proxy firsthand when she was on a hospital clinical rotation long ago.

I totally missed this one, Sarah thought anxiously. *It's the same story. That sweet little boy going slowly downhill with his 'loving mother' standing by his hospital bed...his sad mother, basking in all the attention and sympathy she had been receiving because of her gravely ill child...and then the outpouring of sympathy after his death, just one hour before a lab test came back positive for cyanide and digitalis.*

Sarah could not even imagine how much genuine sympathy and heart-felt attention Jessica would receive if her DD collapsed and died on stage at the upcoming Worlds. 'Munchausen Syndrome by Proxy' monster mothers thrived on attention.

$\mathcal{T}$he Letter-Writer had heard groups of The Others gossiping about their T.C.R.G.'s immoral behavior. *Where* had all of those ridiculous rumors come from?

Before Sylvia's long discourse at the McDonald's, she knew well that she had not written anything even close to the bizarre rumors which had taken on a life of their own. Even so, they were taking their toll on her, just like she had.

After Sylvia had explained defamation to her, she felt like she could breathe again.

Not wanting to interrupt Sylvia's speech, she had crept away to use the Ladies' Room.

At first, she had been confused when she woke up on the floor. Then, after she discovered that her lawyer had left, she had been furious, thinking she had been abandoned and left for dead by her own attorney.

Sylvia had called her later that morning to explain to her client that she would have certainly been 'outed' as the school's Letter-Writer by one of the EMTs, who was, ironically, a dance mom from their own school— *if* her alert attorney had remained by her client's side and had not left the premises immediately.

It was obvious to the Letter-Writer, that she had retained a windy, but nonetheless competent attorney. She would definitely be making a cameo appearance in a future novel....

The Week Of
The World Irish Dance
Championships

Sarah was having great difficulty sleeping ever since
the bonding party. How could she sleep knowing what
she did now? Unless of course she was all wrong? But
her mother's intuition told her she was not imagining
that Jessica's daughter, Catelyn, might be dead sooner
than later if she did not do something quickly.

She had called an old friend, who was now a social
worker at the County Family Mental Health Facility,
on the Sunday morning after the party.

Sarah described in great detail the ambivalence and

disinterest Jessica usually displayed regarding both her daughter's precarious physical and mental conditions. How Jessica's daughter was so weak, she could hardly make it through team rehearsals without collapsing. Finally, Sarah told Karen her concerns about the jar of lima beans and the flowering foxglove plants on the floor of the front porch. Her friend agreed to see what she could find out.

Karen Williams, who had never known Sarah to be an alarmist, decided to make an emergency home visit right away. She would tell Jessica that she had received a phone call that her daughter might need intervention services.

After she had interviewed Jessica and her daughter, she would file a report that would hopefully pave the way for a court order for a medical intervention.

"But," her friend had said, "maybe I can do it the old-fashioned way to speed things up. The older I get, the more convinced I become that intervention should happen immediately."

Sarah kept asking herself the same questions over and over: Was it only a strange coincidence there had been foxglove plants growing on Jessica's porch? Had she gone mad suspecting that Jessica was giving her DD raw lima beans to slowly poison her with cyanide?

***

$\mathcal{B}$randi's Voy activity consumed most of her free time during the week leading up to the Worlds. She already had three negative threads going and was considering another one if she could think of a particularly nasty, hate-driven subject to incite the groupies.

Her three younger children were at grandmother's house for their Easter school break. This freed Brandi to concentrate on her Voy Message Forums and her DD, getting both of them ready for the Worlds.

So far, she had started a few Voy sparks, as she had hoped. Now it was almost time to let go and bring on a grassfire. With only a few more days remaining until the Worlds, there was still plenty of time to bide her own time.

She had calculated that, if she launched her attack in four days, by the time the Worlds had begun, her starter fire would be raging like a forest fire on a dry, windy day.

She would begin with: "I *know* who you are and I'm watching you. Be very careful. You thought your lying letter would bother our dancers? You were so wrong! I will be waiting for you at teams and solos where we will kick your butts, after I spit in your face."

"BTW some of your brighter team moms know what you've done and they don't like it. You had better watch your step."

"P.S. Watch the wine consumption at the Worlds, loser. You will need to have your wits about you. That is of course, if you actually have any."

Since the tone of this ugly post might have been interpreted as being somewhat menacing, even though Brandi was only using fairly harmless words to inflict fear and outrage, she had taken the precaution to travel to a neighboring town to use the computers in their public library. There was no point in getting into legal trouble.

***

Michelle took her daughter back to the Urgent Care Clinic for another shot of cortisone. At this visit, she also asked the Clinic to prescribe some anti-anxiety pills for herself, to help her get through the stress of going to the Worlds and having to be in the same room as her ex-husband.

She resented her ex-husband's not taking more of an interest in their daughter's Irish dancing. He had dared to suggest that it was *her* fault because she made it so miserable and uncomfortable when he showed up at Irish dancing events.

***

Melissa, after much pondering, had decided that she would not be ordering matching under-dress-sleeve-protection for her daughter's three solo dresses.

For one thing, she was still broke.

For another thing, the more she brooded about Linda's theory about adjudicators not ringing the bell when dancers' sleeves began sliding off, the crazier it sounded.

Most conspiracy theories were borderline, if not entirely nuts. She had always heard that the only good conspiracy theory was one that was unprovable.

***

Stacey had decided to let her daughter eat three times each day. The Worlds was only one week away. How

112

much weight could she gain in such a short time frame with a stomach that had to be shrunken by now? After all, it was not like the céilí team had to weigh in before a dance competition like wrestlers did. She hoped. Team dancing at the Worlds was uncharted territory for all of the MAIDS but she was almost positive that Irish dancers on teams were not required to weigh in.

***

Linda gave her daughter some unprecedented time off from her activities to "relax." Except for her daily yoga classes and practicing the piano and the final A Team practices and swimming. Since there were now A Team practices every night until the Worlds, hard as she tried, there was no way to fit everything else in.

She very much hoped that her daughter would not lose ground in her gymnastics classes.

***

Valerie had decided to speak to her daughter again— but only to impart important information. Thankfully, Catelin's sunburn had healed well. Her DD finally had the natural bronze skin Valerie had gone to Mexico to get.

The neck lift had been a big success and Valerie had already scheduled herself at the same clinic again for a new, shorter nose next year. She had allotted extra time before next year's Worlds, in case her daughter's tanning history repeated itself, or her nose needed further adjustment.

She had moved forward and had managed, without seeking professional help, to stop wishing that 'Ann' would disappear from the face of the earth.

***

𝒟ana was positive that she was not imagining that her daughter Kaitlin had grown at least two inches since the hormone shots had started.

She had known from the get-go that those arrogant hormone-pushers had been badly mistaken when they had insisted that it was going to take a long time.

Her husband had left her, but she would sort things out after the Worlds.

At least he had taken the twins with him. It would have been next to impossible trying to keep those two occupied while she was struggling with her DD's bad attitude and her own fears and doubts.

She was certain that he feared their daughter would soon be much taller than he was. He would then blame her for deliberately having made that happen.

Therapist Gert had stabilized her shattered nerves by pointing out that her husband had serious maturity problems and was acting like an adolescent jerk who had to be "taller than the girl."

She asked a few questions about their sex life, but since Dana could not remember the last time that had happened, Therapist Gert had changed the subject.

***

𝒮ylvia concentrated on getting her DD ready for the upcoming weekend's event and making phone calls to her client, the Letter-Writer.

She had not started doing more legal research yet because she was waiting until the Worlds was over so

114

she could concentrate better on points of law and not be so preoccupied with her daughter's dancing results.

She gave Caytlin daily pep talks about how not to be too hopeful that she might be subbed in.

"It was just not going to happen. End of subject. Concentrate on your solo steps," Sylvia chanted each night over and over, in her litany of Sub advice.

***

Social Worker Karen Williams had responded quickly to her friend Sarah's urgent request to investigate a child in need of protective services.

Karen 'borrowed' Susanne Brett, a detective on staff at the Public Defender's Office, to accompany her on what she hoped would turn out to be a one-on-one interview with the young dancer Sarah was so concerned about.

Without having waited for a search warrant signed by a judge, Karen knew she was way out of line. At least she had called Jessica about coming to do a home study in a few weeks to throw her off base.

Worst scenario: if the mother was home, she would try to distract her while Susanne gathered evidence. If Jessica started trouble, Karen would say that she had mixed up the dates and attempt to converse with her. Detective Brett needed time to gather evidence while she interviewed Jessica and the child.

Susanne hoped that she might be able to get the proper paperwork in time because, as she told Sarah, "Good things happen to good people just like bad things happen to good people."

Karen made a few phone calls and was fortunate to have found an adjunct botany professor at the local regional college. Harry Hyde confirmed that Karen's pharmacist friend might be on to something about her toxic lima beans cyanide theory.

He then told Karen something almost too good to be true—that fava beans, *vicia faba*, also called broad beans, looked like lima beans and were very nutritious. He suggested, when she had outlined her concerns, that perhaps fava beans could be switched with the lima beans. Even better, he said he could provide her with enough beans to fill up a large Mason Jar because he was presently teaching a Master Gardener class for adults working towards a Certificate of Horticulture.

It had been decided that Karen would stake out the house from across the street on Tuesday morning.

When Jessica left—and who knew when, or if that would happen as she apparently homeschooled, Karen would immediately call Susanne, who worked in the Public Defender's Office only a few blocks away.

The plan was somewhat elaborate: Jessica leaves. Two leafleting missionaries from a fabricated church go to house and knock on door.

If the daughter does not answer, they go in. If the front door is locked, Susanne has her toolbox in her pocket. If subject daughter is sleeping, they wake her up and explain that God has sent them. She will be surprised but hopefully, not alarmed.

***

Bonne chance joined the team on Tuesday when they

undertook the home visit. Karen had waited for three hours in her cold Ford Escort before she saw subject Jessica walk out of the house carrying Aldi's shopping bags and drive off.

They would have some time.

When the 'missionaries' rang the doorbell, Jessica's frail-looking daughter, opened the front door without a word and let them come in. Karen made a mental note to give this girl a much needed stranger talk.

Soon after they entered, Detective Brett apologized for asking to use their bathroom. Instead, she quietly walked into the kitchen and switched the lima beans Mason Jar with an identical, lidless jar containing the professor's fava beans.

Hopefully, Jessica would not notice the substitution and would continue feeding her daughter the safe fava beans.

Susanne, now wearing white cotton gloves, bagged Jessica's lidless Mason Jar of lima beans and placed it upright in her oversized evidence tote.

She was careful to make sure that the new jar of fava beans was in the exact same place she had found the lima beans. She was indebted to The Hon. Rebecca Roberts for having promptly signed the last minute Search Warrant she had drafted and left on the Judge's busy desk.

Next, Susanne found the pottery with the foxglove plants on a windowsill over the kitchen sink and cut a small leaf from each of the plants.

Finally, she photographed the pottery and the new

Mason Jar without a lid, which was now full of fava beans.

Before she had bagged the lima beans jar, she had placed it next to the fava beans to make sure their bean levels matched. She removed some of the fava beans for balance, and quickly rejoined Karen and Catelyn in the living room.

The women had tried not to wince when they saw how pale and undernourished Catelyn looked. Karen removed a nutrition bar from her tote, apologizing for being rude, while at the same time, asking if Catelyn wanted to share some with her.

Catelyn nodded eagerly and extended her hand for her piece.

Karen casually said, "You know, our Church of the Holy Health believes that people's bodies have to be well-nourished to worship properly. I have a stockpile of these nutrition bars at home."

As she chewed, she rummaged through the bag like she did not already know that there were three dozen other bars in there.

"It's our church's policy to distribute nutrition for the soul and body when they send us out in the field. Here, take these boxes of soul bars I have in my bag, but don't eat them too quickly. Nibble on them, or you might get a tummy ache."

Catelyn was already overjoyed with the contraband food she had just been handed by one stranger when the other stranger said, "You know what? I have a 12-pack of vanilla flavored Ensure in my bag. Here, take it. I have lots more back at the Church."

Catelyn was beyond happy. Karen then pulled out a carton of Boost Very High Calorie Drinks for Kids that she had managed to stuff into her bag and handed it to Catelyn.

Karen and Susanne, knowing that Catelyn would probably never do this, urged her to, "Be sure to tell your parents to come to our church sometime."

Catelyn smiled and thanked them. She said that she hoped they would stop in again soon for another visit and urged them to bring more soul food if they could.

***

Catelyn closed the front door and raced upstairs to her room. She hid the nutritional supplements in her closet, under the floor boards she had loosened years ago.

As instructed, she nibbled on the next nutrition bar and savored every sip of a vanilla Ensure. It was hard not to wolf down the delicious food. Especially since she was now listening carefully for the return of her mother.

She knew well that she could not afford to have her mother discover the food or the food wrappers, or any evidence whatsoever of visitors, as it could be bad for her.

Very bad for her.

She winced, remembering the time her mother had kept her in the hall closet all day when she had taken a shower without asking for permission.

119

*W*hen Detective Brett got back to her cubicle, she immediately drafted a 'Child In Need Of Protective Services,' and an Arrest Warrant for Jessica Reynolds, to be served immediately—which could mean as long as next Monday morning after the staff attorney and a judge had signed them.

At least they had managed to switch the beans and left Catelyn enough food to sustain her until she could be removed from the house.

Susanne Brett had a bad feeling about Jessica. She took her pressing concerns to the District Attorney's Office later that afternoon. After a short consultation, she was assured the Arrest Warrant she had drafted for the D.A.'s signature, would be signed today by Judge Roberts, and that it would be served no later than this Saturday morning. Hopefully sooner.

Karen Williams called Sarah and left a message that things were in progress and not to worry.

She had removed the lima beans and replaced them with fava beans and left boxes of nutritional snacks and shakes.

Most importantly, Detective Brett was going to get warrants signed by a judge and served before Catelyn's precarious health deteriorated any further.

***

*W*as Jessica imagining it, or was her daughter starting to look better?

She was positive that Sarah was the informer who

had called the Child Welfare Unit.

Had she also been sneaking food to her daughter? From now on, she would watch Sarah closely.

She would make Sarah pay dearly for that "child in need of protective services" phone call.

Social Services had said that they would be coming to the house in three weeks for an interview.

Evidently, Sarah had not made her call sound like there was something life or death going on.

The stupid cow.

Jessica packed an extra big handful of beans for her DD's final dance rehearsal later that night.

She would harvest the pink foxglove flowers early tomorrow morning. Before little Catelyn got in her face and distracted her.

***

*S*arah had been anxiously waiting to hear back from Karen as to when the paperwork would be served on Jessica.

So far, there had been no new updates.

The MAIDS and DDs were leaving for the Worlds the next morning at 10:45 on their chartered minibus.

Tonight was the last pre-competition team practice.

She had very much hoped that Jessica would have been arrested and in a jail cell before the team set off.

At team practices over the last three days, Catelyn had looked noticeably healthier and had considerably more energy.

Karen's phone call had definitely rattled Jessica. She seemed to be very agitated, mumbling and sometimes whistling Jingle Bells.

She hand-fed a few fava beans to her DD at every break—like she was feeding a baby animal at a petting zoo.

It was easy to see that Jessica's confusion and anger were accelerating as she watched her DD dancing with more energy and enthusiasm at each practice.

It had been a very draining week for Sarah.

Jessica's eyes had probed at her like Sauron looking for the Ring.

Had Jessica seen her looking at the foxglove plants on the porch?

She must have—because Jessica knew.

Arrival
The Day Before
The World Irish Dance
Championships

*W*hen the comfortable minibus that the MAIDS had engaged to transport them to the World Irish Dance Championships, approached the ginormous complex hosting the supersized event, they did not notice.

The panic Sarah had created when she had stopped stirring her Bloody Mary and said, "So then, none of us know what the name of our competition is?" was contagious.

Sarah, by far the calmest of the MAIDS and usually their moderator when things got overheated, had been unable to convince the group that they might not find a listing for a U-13 8-Hand Céilí A Team in their programs because it was probably going to be called either a Junior Girls Figure 13-16, a Minor Girls Figure

U-13, a Junior Girls Céilí 13-16 or a Minor Girls Céilí 11-13.

She had also pointed out, that calling it the 'A' Team was silly because their school did not have a 'B' Team. The MAIDS had attached the letter 'A' only to make the team sound important—big-league.

"There is not going to be an 'A' Team because our school does *not have* a 'B' Team!" Sarah said over and over, totally exasperated by the MAIDS' stubbornness.

The hysteria caused by the uncertainty was getting out-of-hand and some of the MAIDS were screaming as they argued with each other, causing the bus driver to pull over to the side of the long entrance driveway's curb and ask them to please, "keep it down!"

Sarah had to admit that she too was very confused by everything except the 'Letter A.'

Their T.C.R.G. had apparently deliberately missed the minibus which had created an atmosphere of fear of the unknown and mass insecurity. The TC's phone had been turned off and it was not taking messages.

The MAIDS felt like they had been cut off, severed from the Mother Ship, orbiting Planet Earth in their pilotless space capsule. They were totally on their own.

What if she were not going to show up? Ever.

The TC had been wearing large sunglasses at the school ever since the letter fiasco. None of them had been able to look directly into her eyes to get a good reading on her mental condition. She had not entirely abandoned everything, but had not bothered helping their team to prepare for the Worlds.

She mostly just sat in her office, probably staring, but no one could tell for certain underneath her dark shades.

Even so, none of the MAIDS had expected her to be a 'No Show' for the minibus to the WORLDS! Not so much as one phone call, apologizing or explaining why she was now too crazy to join them.

The unthinkable had happened to the MAIDS. It was painfully clear, that it was entirely up to them now, to navigate the uncharted waters waiting to drown them at the World Irish Dance Championships.

First, it would be necessary to find out what their competition numbers were.

On the bright side, none of The Others' DDs had qualified for the Worlds, so they were not going to be hanging around them. There was already more than enough on the MAIDS' plates.

When the level of nerves had almost reached the meltdown point, worse news was announced by Linda. She had texted a mom from another dance school and, without admitting to her friend that she had no idea which competition her own DD's team was entered into, because she was calling on a borrowed phone and did not want to talk long, she asked her friend to look it up for her.

Linda's friend came through immediately and the MAIDS were high fiving until they had processed all of the new information. Their DDs' team, entered in whatever Linda said it was being called at the Worlds, danced tomorrow at the *first round—first!* U-13 solo steps were scheduled all afternoon and then again, the day after tomorrow. All of the MAIDS had agreed that they would worry about the solo steps, after their team had danced.

What if their team recalled?

Were there team recalls at the Worlds?

Where was that fugitive tramp who called herself their TC?

It was going to be humiliating asking someone else what to do all the time. They would have to take turns gathering information as they went along, so as not to broadcast to the Worlds that they were really a bunch of clueless losers.

This having the first-up-slot-in-the-morning news was very distressing. There would be the team practice tonight, possibly in the hotel lobby if their TC had not reserved a rehearsal room, and then it would have to be straight to bed afterwards.

When the distressing "first team up" news reached the back of the bus, the DDs, who had been sleeping for the past three hours, woke up.

The confusing schedule information was followed by another logical question. When Linda asked where they were all going to sleep that night, there was dead silence. Each of the MAIDS looked around hopefully at one another, searching for the reservation maker.

Eventually, it dawned on them that their T.C.R.G., who was still unreachable, had told Stacey last week that she had found the best possible hotel and booked it for them.

Jessica questioned Stacey about it savagely, but she remained adamant about the TC not having told her the name of their hotel.

Just that it was one of the best hotels.

Sylvia stepped in before Jessica got out of control and suggested that they start calling the "best hotels," asking if there was a reservation for a) their school, or b) in their T.C.R.G.'s name.

An online search quickly revealed that there were over a hundred hotels and motels in the vicinity. Sylvia started phoning reservation desks near the Worlds' complex.

"Well this is just great!" said Valerie. "Where are we supposed to do make-up? In a public restroom?"

"Who cares about make-up, Valerie?" a chorus of fearful MAIDS asked, aware that that there were more important things to worry about at the moment.

Valerie was about to defend her important make-up concerns when she was interrupted by an avalanche of worse fears: "Where are we going to sleep tonight? We are like a small army and every hotel room within miles is already booked—including our own rooms, wherever they might be."

"This is the WORLDS, for God's sake, not some small hick feis in the middle of a cornfield! Don't you get it? There *are* no rooms—at least not enough for all of us."

"We have got to find our TC!" Linda insisted.

"Who knows where she lives?"

After considerable mumbling it was clear that none

of the MAIDS had any idea where she lived.

"Maybe we should call the local Red Cross?" Stacey suggested. "They help people who become displaced after disasters." No one responded.

"The girls are supposed to rehearse tonight in one of the hotel conference rooms. Now I wonder if *it* was reserved?" Melissa said, mostly to herself.

Sylvia, sick of being put on hold and then hung up on by rude hotel reservation staffs like she was some kind of nutcase, spoke up:

"This is a BIG human interest news story, ladies. I am going to call around to all the TV stations with our predicament. It could be likened to the 'looking for a room in Bethlehem' story."

"The media will immediately respond and send an eager, most likely a rookie, woman reporter, who will make live, on-location, broadcast appeals, asking for shelter for Irish dancers and their mothers. It will be a nice filler piece for their television station. We could have the girls do their Slip Jig."

"Are you crazy?" Dana shouted.

"We are supposed to go to a bunch of strangers' houses? Get a grip, Sylvia! Who is going to have twenty extra sleeping places for us? Except a bordello or den of sick perverts? Don't hold your breath for an acceptable invitation."

Sarah had already contacted the local police in their dance school's vicinity and reported their T.C.R.G. as 'missing.'

"The police said they would try to find her and get

back to us with a report as soon as possible."

"Worst scenario," Sarah continued, "maybe one of the hotels would let us sleep in their lounging chairs around the pool when they close for the night?"

"There would probably be the reclining kind. And if all the hotels in the complex refuse, *then* we call the local television stations?"

The DDs in the back of the bus thought this was by far the best plan—like a pool slumber party.

They conversed in enthusiastic, quiet voices about how, when all of their MAIDS had consumed enough of whatever alcohol they would be drinking in their poolside chairs and had fallen asleep, they could jump in the pool and swim all night!

The entire team began lobbying for the reclining poolside chairs idea. They said they thought it was a "brilliant idea."

Linda's daughter was ecstatic. She had been in a state of panic about missing her swim team's practices both today and tomorrow, for the State Swimming and Diving Meet next weekend.

Now she would be able to work on her freestyle stroke all night.

Suddenly, the 'no available rooms reality' seemed like the best thing that could have ever happened and even the MAIDS hoped now that the police would not find their T.C.R.G. who might have actually booked hotel rooms somewhere for all of them.

Nobody wanted to babysit her anyway.

Besides, it had been three weeks since their TC had

even spoken to any of them. She had let the slightly critical letter eat at her insides like a parasitic worm and spoke only in fragmented sentences—if she spoke at all.

They had been rehearsing their céilí without their TC all week, with the MAIDS taking turns drilling the dancers.

Mostly, it had been Jessica drilling, because she had insisted that she was the most qualified.

Having had enough of the MAIDS quibbling with and yelling at each other for the last four hours, the bus driver drove up to the venue's entrance.

He helped the MAIDS and their DDs unload their luggage and then, before anyone had the chance to ask him to wait somewhere close by while they tried to figure out where they were going to be for the night, and what time the next day they would need to be picked up, he floored the bus accelerator and sped away from the 'Drop Off Only' curb, disappearing into an ocean of traffic.

The MAIDS hardly noticed as they stood together, united, gazing at the formidable network of connected buildings which was enabling their wildest dreams for their daughters to take place in less than twenty-four hours.

It no longer seemed to matter that they had no idea where they would all be sleeping that night, and to the amazement of their DDs, they walked along joyfully, like they were following the Yellow Brick Road to Oz. They were not linking arms like Dorothy did with her three friends, but they moved along together, a unified front, with a single objective.

Finding the Worlds' Information Desk to get maps and stage assignments tuned out to be easy-peasy, and their daughters were officially checked in at the World Irish Dance Championships without a glitch.

Everything seemed to be under control.

***

Sarah was exhausted from constantly keeping both eyes fixed on Jessica.

She had warned her daughter to keep away from that evil witch, but how did one tell Jessica's child that her own mother was plotting to murder her?

Sarah watched Jessica's every move and gesture. It was going to be a long, long Worlds.

***

The MAIDS pooled their loose cash and generously bribed the night security guard they had met patrolling the hallway next to one of the more 'out of the way' swimming pools.

Officer 'Smith,' who told them she too had an eight-year-old dancer, said it would be no problem looking the other way all night as she made her rounds. She had started her shift four hours early today because the regular guard had left with flu symptoms. She would be on duty until 6:30 tomorrow morning.

Before continuing on her rounds, Officer 'Smith' showed the MAIDS how to lock themselves in from the inside. It was a comfortable arrangement for all of the parties concerned.

There were twenty-five reclining poolside chairs and the pool room was pleasantly warm.

***

*A*fter the Team had gone through their céilí five times in the large conference room that their T.C.R.G. had remembered to reserve, the MAIDS thought the team could not get any better.

Their daughters looked like world champions.

While the girls were doing their cool-downs, Sarah had, on a hunch, found the team's picnic basket in the pile of suitcases and dress carriers by the door and set off to explore.

Only one conference room away, she discovered a small 'Employees Only' breakroom that had a large microwave oven and a small microwave oven.

Sarah furiously began microwaving the MAIDS' now defrosted, room temperature egg rolls and the DDs' spaghetti and meatballs unfrozen dinners, using both ovens, hoping that an employee would not come in for a much deserved break.

***

*S*pirits were high in the venue's vast lobby as the DDs feasted on the well-warmed spaghetti and meatball microwave dinners they had brought with them for good luck.

The MAIDS were happily eating soggy vegetarian egg rolls, sipping red wine from three ounce leftover Dixie cups Jessica had packed.

132

At 9:00 p.m., the MAIDS and their DDs started back to the swimming pool.

As promised, the door was unlocked.

The DDs pretended to be very disappointed that their MAIDS had forbidden them to swim until after their competitions were over the next day.

They were very taken aback that their MAIDS had forgotten about having them get spray tanned. They were not going to place in the morning anyway—tanned or otherwise—and would not have been able to swim tonight if they had DHA on their skin.

With protests worthy of an Academy Award, the DDs settled into the sleeping bags they routinely took with them to feiseanna, in the event they might end up sleeping on a hotel room's rug.

Sleeping all night on reclining lounging chairs, next to the dimly lit, pear-shaped swimming pool, would be totally awesome, but the DDs knew that the odds of this ever happening again, were slim to none. They decided that they were going to make the most of this exciting opportunity. Cat nap now and party later.

The DDs knew that their MAIDS were not going to willingly pass out before they did.

A few of the less trusting MAIDS were already suspicious and looked determined to 'wait them out.'

However, the DDs knew that they would be able to outlast their exhausted mothers and were patiently biding their time, pretending to be asleep.

When the MAIDS had consumed enough wine to no longer be able to keep their watchful eyes open, even in slits, they began to perform a symphonic choir piece later titled, "Snoring Sonata" by their irreverent daughters.

The DDs pooled their Worlds money and emptied most of the snacks from the vending machines located in both the men's and women's locker rooms.

They drank Coke and Pepsi and Mountain Dew to get them through the long night ahead.

Except for Linda's daughter, who did laps all night and had declined to enter an all-night Piggyback Team Water Wrestling event, it was a memorable night for the U-13 Team before they danced first thing in the morning.

Five hours later, when it became apparent that all of them were utterly done in, they called it quits and left the pool, after having intercepted Linda's daughter as she swam by them in the shallow end.

Working as a team, they pulled and heaved her up and over the side.

Not having enough energy to look for dry towels, they climbed into their warm sleeping bags and passed out on their comfortable poolside reclining chairs.

It was 4:00 a.m.

The Day Of The World Irish Dance Championships

Totus est puteus ut ends puteus

*A*t precisely six a.m. sharp, the MAIDS' mobile phone alarms sounded in unison and a deluge of happy 'good morning' wakeup music assaulted their stupefied DDs.

Mercifully, the MAIDS were blissfully unaware that

their 'soon to be World Champions' had only had two hours of sleep.

Linda's daughter was back in the pool, swimming laps again. Her mother smiled, proud of the incredible work ethic she had installed in her daughter. She had no idea that her DD had been swimming for most of last night, getting ready for next weekend.

Today, it was the Irish dance championships. Next Saturday, it would be the swim team championships. Linda had always thought that a laurel wreath crown had been placed on her tiny newborn daughter's head before the umbilical cord had been cut.

The rest of the U-13 8-Hand Céilí Team dancers staggered to the bathroom, where they leaned against the cool tiled walls, trying to trick themselves back to life.

Brandi set off to find coffee, not so much to get caffeine in her system, but to eavesdrop on groups of early risen MAIDS from schools all over the world.

It occurred to her, walking slowly down the long hallway leading to the competition areas, that she had only planted her rotten seeds on English-speaking Voy Boards, so she would be limited to her own tongue.

She hoped that the other MAIDS here today who spoke English, but who could also speak Irish Gaelic and some of the other Celtic languages, would stick to plain English. It would be a real pity to miss out on bitchiness because of a language barrier.

There was also the snag that, although English was normally the language spoken in most of Ireland and in Northern Ireland, Scotland, Wales, Cornwall and obviously, England, she had discovered she had great difficulty understanding their heavy 'foreign' accents. Especially the way the Scots always burred their 'r' sounds and some of the Irish seemed to gasp and then speak in tongues. It would make eavesdropping in the hallways difficult.

Here in her own country, she also often had trouble following Stacey with her ridiculous, mushy Southern drawl and Linda's clipped New England words.

Specifically, she was hoping to discover pockets of uptight women who looked edgy and angry. She had not been able to do much sleuthing the night before.

She became almost euphoric, when she paused by a drinking fountain and heard a strident voice yelling, "Will you please get over yourself! Who told you we came here just to kick your butts?"

Things got even better when a small audience of mostly 40ish women had appeared from nowhere, like roaches in a NYC apartment when the kitchen lights are suddenly switched on, to watch what they hoped might prove to be an interesting slap down event.

"You know very well that we're the ones who are always kicking *your* butts!" another MAID observed. "Can you remember one single time when we did not make your sorry asses look pathetic?"

After the word "pathetic," it got better. There were approximately four separate groups of women who had begun using most of the words and terms found in Brandi's Voy Dictionary-Thesaurus. It was like they had taken a college level course from her: Introduction to Basic Insults.

To make sure things continued to intensify, Brandi entered into the fracas: "You sleazy THOTS, now I know who you are. So which one of you wrote that letter?"

Brandi was thrilled to see that a few of the women seemed to be to backing off, sneaking away. It was now obvious to Brandi that the Letter scandal at her school had spread far and wide. She had thought from the beginning that the Letter might have been written by someone from another school trying to put a chink in an untested school's armor.

Sylvia had obviously made up the whole outlandish story about the 'confession' in the bathroom. And the dimwitted MAIDS had all fallen for it. *Serves them right*, she thought bitterly. Her Katelynne would be avenged after all. *Sub #2 my ass....*

"That's it, just sneak away, you snot-nosed cowards, because you'll never admit what you did. Don't think you are the only sleazeballs who have tried to do this to us!"

When no one replied, Brandi said: "That's what I figured. You're just a bunch of hissing sluts. I have no time for trolls."

With this final remark, she strode off, following the inviting aroma of morning coffee. Brandi had done well so far, but she had many more little campfires to ignite. Behind her, she was happy to hear the noise level accelerating into fourth gear.

***

$\mathcal{L}$inda's daughter at first refused to get out of the pool. She said she had to keep practicing her freestyle stroke and would much rather swim than eat. When she was reminded that they had all been sleeping illegally in the hotel's pool area, with open hours clearly posted, she reluctantly climbed out, threw on her unworn pajamas and stuffed her wet Speedo into her overnight bag.

It was already 6:15 a.m. The team would be dancing at 8:00 a.m. sharp. With all their luggage and dress carriers, the MAIDS and their DDs looked like they had just arrived at the Worlds when they claimed their little corner of the lobby and slumped down into a section of comfortable chairs and small couches.

Most of the DDs said they were far too nervous to eat, but it was actually because they were still stuffed with vending machine potato chips and chocolate bars and crackers with fake cheese. All they really wanted to do was to catch some more sleep while they waited.

The two MAIDS who had gone to great lengths to find the Room Service Office and explain their sad situation about not actually having rooms where food could be delivered, had managed to bring forty plain donuts, twenty orange juice cartons, ten small cartons of milk and ten large coffees, back with them—after tipping 150% of the bill and arguing unsuccessfully for fresh fruit and protein.

All ten of the DDs looked rough from sleeping in the pool area, and make-up was being discussed when the food and drinks arrived, transported triumphantly into the now packed lobby by Sylvia and Melissa.

The DDs did not mind any of the inconveniences they had endured so far. Swimming all night, gorging on forbidden snacks and then two whole donuts each for breakfast?

They would never have even *though*t of asking for a breakfast donut at an Oireachtas, let alone the Worlds.

Two whole donuts? It was an almost unbelievable development.

So far, this entire trip to the World Championships had been nothing short of amazing for the exhausted DDs.

It was already 7:00 a.m. and time—way *past* time, to do makeup and wigs in the lobby restroom. Back in their tiny corner alcove again, the MAIDS formed a protective circle, shielding their DDs, as they slipped into their U-13 Team costumes.

The MAIDS cooperated with one another as they inspected ghillies and hard shoes. Sarah applied duct tape to several ragged ankles under new poodle socks.

Most importantly, the MAIDS hoped their DDs had been able to conjure up a, 'We're Number One' attitude, no matter how far-fetched it now seemed, before they met their dancing destiny.

***

*J*t was 7:45. Both Subs were now wearing their team dresses, in the now extremely unlikely event that they were going to be called upon to fill in for one of the regular team members.

The sleep-walking DDs and their weary MAIDS,

walked into the huge ballroom, gaping at the stage at the far end of the room where their fate at the Worlds was soon going to be determined.

There was a long table on the floor in front of the stage. Adjudicators were sitting there, sipping coffee and juice and acting normally, as if the world was not about to end.

Five of the U-13 Team counted three adjudicators. The other three said that there were at least four. Had the team forgotten how to count? How were they ever going to get through this? Was counting people the same as counting music while dancing? All of them needed to be able to *count* doing their céilí. They were doomed.

When the stage monitor beckoned to them, they began mechanically moving towards the front of the room with feet that seemed now to weigh more than their torsos.

Approximately fifty feet from the stage, Michelle's daughter let out a heart-stopping scream and fell to the floor, shrieking. Holding her knee, which appeared to have popped out of place, she was in agony.

Michelle, who was sitting with the MAIDS in the tenth row, jumped up and, in complete denial, ran to her daughter and tried to pull her back up on to her feet, shouting, "NO! You cannot do this *now*, don't you understand? Not NOW! You GOT the shot! Just ten more minutes, then you can scream all you want to!"

While Michelle kept violently tugging, and her DD kept screaming and crying, a concerned looking man ran over from the audience and knelt down on the floor next to his daughter. He cradled her with his left arm, while trying to keep Michelle from pulling his child up with his right.

A prim looking young woman appeared at his side, and attempted to assist him in preventing his ex-wife from pulling their hysterical daughter up to her feet.

In slow motion, Michelle finally let go of her DD and lunged at the prim woman who was trying to help her ex-husband keep her away from her own child.

She pounced on the harlot like a wild cat. Like she was representing all of the trusting, married women on earth who had been betrayed by their philandering husbands. Michelle fully intended to pull the younger woman's blonde hair out, root by root, as she tackled the whore, intermittently slapping and punching her in the face.

Two obviously nervous security officers rushed in to break up the unprecedented bitch fight. They were followed by Worlds' paramedics pushing a gurney for the downed dancer.

The male security guard tried to separate the ladies on the floor. The female security guard the MAIDS had bribed the night before, tried to keep a low profile, fearing her last night's indiscretion might be reported if she made the MAIDS angry by trying to help the wrong woman.

While the male security guard was trying to get the aggressive, slapper-attacker off the lady on the floor, two sheriff's deputies, having been informed that their arrest warrant must be served before the first team danced at the Worlds on Saturday morning in the main auditorium, moved purposefully up the middle aisle, loudly announcing that they needed to "speak with Jessica Reynolds."

This caused Jessica, who had been shadowing the dancers on their way up to the stage, to try to escape by pushing aside the team dancers and shoving her BPA-free thermos containing her deadly foxglove tea, at her DD, the U-13 Team Captain, who was leading the procession.

While Jessica was ordering her DD to "drink the stamina tea" before they danced, Sarah dislodged the thermos from Jessica's long fingers and Jessica took off running. The two deputies quickly apprehended the crazed, runaway MAID.

While she was being handcuffed by the deputies, Jessica demanded that her thermos be returned to her immediately, insisting her daughter was gravely ill and might collapse if she did not have her special tea.

Sarah handed the thermos to one of the deputies, and explained that she was a licensed pharmacist, and was positive the thermos contained herbal tea that was poisoned with foxglove and would quickly kill anyone who took so much as one sip.

She could not help but notice that the deputy was looking at her like she had two heads.

The handcuffed Jessica, spewing expletives like a lawn sprinkler as the deputies tried unsuccessfully to convince her to walk, caused parents of the dancers in the audience to cover their children's ears.

While the County Sheriff's deputies were trying to take Jessica away peacefully, City Police came running in to arrest Michelle for assault and battery.

Michelle's daughter was pushed away on a gurney, crying less hysterically now, after having had her knee wrapped and a local sedative administered. She was followed by her father and his bruised, prim-looking girlfriend, who was being carried on a stretcher, and Michelle in handcuffs, repeatedly referring to her ex-husband as, "that slimy bastard!"

The leftover MAIDS were afraid of how the Jessica trauma might have affected her daughter, Catelyn.

They need not have worried. Catelyn had found a cardboard pizza box on an empty chair on the way up to the stage and was busy stuffing the leftover pieces into her mouth.

The two sheriff's deputies, having been unable to convince their lady prisoner to walk, had finally lifted Jessica up by her elbows, between them. With her feet only inches off the ground, she seemed to float down the aisle, like a bad angel who had found a portal up from hell.

There was a bell ringing in the hands of a female adjudicator who politely asked if the Team was ready to proceed now.

MAID Valerie looked ready to do battle should the same adjudicator *not* ring the same bell if one of the team members' dresses malfunctioned.

The MAIDS were amazed that those of them who

had not been arrested seemed so unruffled by all that had just happened.

Maybe there really was a dress conspiracy? After all, did not an adjudicator just *ring a bell?*

Sylvia almost went into shock when she realized that it would be her daughter, Sub #1, who would be replacing Michelle's over-cortisoned Katelyn.

Sub # 1, who had already laced up her ghillies, gave her mother a confident peck on the cheek and walked, head held high, up the side aisle towards the stage.

After the U-13 8-Hand Céilí Team finally reached backstage, they discovered that Linda's daughter had not accompanied them. No one had noticed that she was missing.

The ensuing panic depleted the confidence that the disoriented dancers had somehow managed to gather on their journey to the stage, until Brandi's daughter, Sub #2, appeared backstage.

"She'll be okay, I think she overdid the swimming thing. She's out on the floor in the hallway, sucking on her thumb. But I'm totally ready for this!"

"Let's just walk out there and get this stupid thing over with!"

Sarah was so stunned, that she was never quite sure afterwards exactly what had all happened. Whether it had been a comedy or tragedy. It had seemed like a bit of both.

Michelle, was being read her *Miranda* Rights as she passed by Linda, who was out in the hallway, sobbing and leaning on her dazed husband, following behind the EMTs pushing the gurney holding their beloved, strapped-down daughter, in the fetal position, sucking her thumb.

Sarah's friend, Karen Williams, had shown up with a handsome, middle aged man that she introduced as Doctor Paul Potenza, Jessica's estranged husband who was also Catelyn's father. He happily announced that he was going to take her home with him to New Jersey right after the Worlds.

Doctor Potenza was planning to file for permanent custody. Karen had discovered that Jessica was still legally married to this man, who had been told by his wife, three years after he had fled from her after she had tried to poison him with cyanide, that she had obtained a divorce due to his 'desertion' of her.

She had then dropped the bomb that the daughter he had never known about was now three years old. She promised him that she would make sure that he would never see his child.

For years he had tried to locate his daughter, not even sure that she actually existed, but Jessica, whose real name was 'Adele Anderson,' had moved several times, taking great care to hide her real identity, and had somehow managed to get another Social Security number with the name, Jessica Reynolds.

This is a crazy soap opera, Sarah thought, as another adjudicator rang a bell, alerting the eight lovely Irish dancers standing two by two in a large circle, center stage, arms rigidly down by their sides, that it was time for Team Captain Catelyn to prepare her 8-Hand U-

13 Céilí Team for take-off.

'Trip to the Cottage' music started.

The Team counted. The MAIDS held their breath.

Dana's too-short daughter quite effortlessly made contact with Sylvia's daughter's hand and together, they lifted their clasped hands shoulder level, pointed their right toes, and moved off gracefully, weaving and spinning in and out of the céilí circle.

The U-13 8-Hand Céilí Team danced flawlessly and their new Team dresses' sleeves remained intact.

It had not been necessary for an adjudicator *not* to ring a bell.

***

"*N*ever seen *anything* like it," an awe-struck security guard said, standing in the hallway with another guard many hours later. "It was epic."

"First team's up at 8:00 a.m. and it's like a bar room free-for-all in there. I could have sold tickets. I had to guard this door, so I didn't have hands-on close ups, but I saw plenty from back here."

"Some years ago, a mother at one of them twirling competitions, got out of line when a baton flew at her kid and smacked her little twirler in the face. She took it personally. The mom I mean, not the injured twirler. That twirler was a little trooper. She just handed that loose baton back to the other twirler and both of them kept smiling and twirling away while their raging dance moms were being escorted out of the auditorium."

"But that incident was nothing. Not even close to what you missed right here, first thing this morning."

147

The second shift guard exhaled, regretting his bad luck at having been scheduled for a boring shift that would consist of patrolling the first level hallways and securely locking competition areas up for the night.

"There were sheriff's deputies holding up one lady in handcuffs, trying to get her to walk out peacefully down the center aisle. Something was just 'off' about that one. She looked like some kind of creep-you-out snake, writhing around and sticking out her tongue—cussing worse than my Uncle Ted."

"Anyway, at the same time, some of our local police were bringing another so-called lady out in handcuffs, right down this side aisle where we're standing now. She had taken some other lady down to the floor and started punching and slapping at her."

"The lady who was down on the floor, the one who was being beaten by the lady in handcuffs, before she had them on of course, passed out and she had to be rushed out on a stretcher by our medics."

"One screaming dancer is down on the floor inside the ballroom with a dislocated knee. Another one out here in the hall, is on the floor, curled up like a baby, sucking on her thumb."

"And the thumb-sucker's parents are yelling at each other about whose fault *was* this? Their kid's down on the floor sucking her thumb and they're blaming each other. It was amazing."

$\mathcal{T}$hirteen hours later, following two nail-biting recalls, the U-13 8-Hand Céilí Team was on stage, along with two other teams at the Awards Ceremony.

Long blue ribbons, with dangling First Place Gold Medals, were placed over each of their bobbing heads. The far more experienced, second and third runners-up teams, tried not to display their incredulity at this unexpected development.

This first place team did not even seem to have a T.C.R.G. Who *were* they?

And who was that weird "Gert" lady who had been standing behind them the whole time while they were waiting for results, going on and on about "centering" and "harnessing the power of the universe?"

The U-13 8-Hand Céilí Team dancers, who had also done their solo steps, did not recall in either their hard shoe or soft shoe competitions, but were far too happy to dwell on it.

It remained an open question as to whether or not the 'sliding sleeves' conspiracy theory was valid, since

Worlds dancers' dress sleeves had remained intact and so far, there had been no obvious dress malfunctions.

***

a woman dressed in black, wearing large sunglasses, stood outside the ballroom doors, closely observing the Awards Ceremony and eating M&Ms. She stayed back, lest the MAIDS spot her, and wondered why none of them had checked into the five rooms she had reserved here at the hotel for them.

By the time the World Champion First Place U-13 8-Hand Céilí Team Dancers, had finished posing for pictures and visiting with their new fans and families, the woman dressed in black, wearing large sunglasses and eating M&Ms, had vanished.

THE END ?

LIST OF ILLUSTRATIONS

Cover: Attic Greek Vase. **Detail of Medusa fleeing from Perseus.** "Berlin Painter." Red figure potters. 490 BC. Museum Collection. Antikensammlungen, Munich.

Title Page: Harpy. Sketch of vase detail. Unknown

Dedication: Modern sketch of Nine Muses. Unknown

Poetry Page: Medusa. Artist: Caravaggio

Page 1: Medusa. Sketch: Jnerson Mythology Project

Page 5: Medusa. Artist: Elihu Vedder 1867

Page 11: Medusa. Artist: Vincenzo Gemito

Page 13: Medusa Bust. Sculptor: Bernini

Page 19: Medusa. Artist: Unknown

Page 25: Medusa. Artist: Franz Von Stuck

Page 29: Medusa. Artist: Arnold Bocklin

Page 33: Goddess Hera. Sculptor: Barberini

Page 37: Medusa. Artist: Frederick Sandys

Page 41: Medusa. Artist: Jacques Wagrez

Page 49: Calliope. Muse of Epic Poetry. Unknown

Page 53: Five Muses. Ancient bas-relief (highlighted)

151

ABOUT THE AUTHOR

Brenna Briggs is the author of
THE LIFFEY RIVERS IRISH DANCER
MYSTERIES
www.liffeyrivers.com

Other Books By Brenna Briggs

The Mystery of the Sparkling Solo Dress Crown
The Mystery of the Winking Judge
The Secret of the Mountain of the Moon
In the Shadow of the Serpent
The Alaskan Sun
The Mystery of the Pointing Dog
Four Mini Mysteries

Made in the USA
Lexington, KY
18 January 2017